I0709211

This is a work of fiction. Names, characters, places, and incidents either are the product of the author's imagination or are used fictitiously. Any resemblance to actual events, locales, organizations, or persons, living or dead, is entirely coincidental and beyond the intent of either the author or the publisher.

3

A Gentleman of Substance
by Julia Talbot

A Gentleman of Substance

Chapter One

Virginia 1803

I mean no offense to you at all, Madeline, but this must be the most excruciating event I've ever attended. I cannot imagine anything duller."

Smoothing the outdated beauty patch on her cheek back into place, Madeline looked Michael sidelong and her painted lips stretched into a thin smile. "Well, I did warn you that this was neither Boston nor Philadelphia."

"My dear, this is not merely provincial. It is positively barbaric." Michael was fairly certain Madeline would not take umbrage with his statement, and, indeed, she offered only a slight shrug of her bony shoulders. Another displaced member of high society, thanks to her husband's agricultural bent, the lady could easily understand his ire at his unwilling banishment to this backwoods hellhole.

"You have no one to blame but yourself," she pointed out, arching one thinly-drawn brow at him.

Oh, and was that not the truth? Not that Michael would ever admit it aloud, at least not to her. Still, she had a point. If only he had learned the hard-won lesson of discretion before he was sent away in disgrace to this tiny corner of Virginia. Sadly, though it perhaps was indeed the better part of valor, discretion had never been his strong suit. Deciding to start immediately upon a campaign to better his familiarity with the word, Michael chose not to answer the accusation and sipped at his brandy instead.

What a lot of boorish, semi-illiterate louts, he thought as he surveyed the room. Yes, he knew that was unfair, because the education these folk had at their disposal differed greatly from his. Yes, he was certainly spoiled by the glittering soirees of New York and Boston. But really, he could go to a tavern in Newport and find better conversationalists than these people. Listening with only half and ear to his companion, Michael amused himself by cataloguing the poor fit of this one's coat or the obvious outline of that one's truss.

"Oh. Oh, my. Who is that?" The grip Madeline had on this arm became suddenly painfully tight, which made Michael return his attention to her.

"What?"

"Look there."

Following the direction of Madeline's pointing fan, Michael looked. Oh, my, indeed. Clothed in a rather old-fashioned coat of deep blue, with equally unusual gray and silver breeches and hose, the gentleman in question removed his hat and handed it to the servant just inside the door. Tall, well-built, with hair the color of walnut heartwood pulled back into a severe club at the base of his neck, the fellow was truly a magnificent specimen. He was brown as a nut from being in the sun, with tiny lines that crinkled at the corners of his eyes when he smiled at his hostess, and even from the distance of half the room, Michael saw those eyes were a rich, mossy green.

Michael shifted uncomfortably as his body tightened. Desire shot through him, and his mouth all but watered. Yes, Michael wanted this one badly. So much for his resolution to practice discretion.

"Well, well, Madeline," he said. "You did promise me amusement if I introduced you about. It very well may be that you did not lie to me after all."

Lord above, but Daniel Calhoun despised these confounded affairs. A bunch of corpulent ne'er-do-wells and their women, standing around drinking and gossiping about their neighbors. Men with paint on their faces, of all things. Daniel knew very well that most of these folk thought he was some sort of Puritan, a man who denied himself even the smallest bits of sin. Far from it. He simply preferred his pleasures honest. A strong drink, a hot fire, maybe a good pipe. Maybe an eager partner in his bed for a short time.

That was the trouble with this high-end sort, he thought while he removed his heavy outer coat and hat, handing them to a silently waiting bondsman. Their women weren't soft. They had a hardness about them, a brittle demeanor that never failed to unnerve him. No matter that he had not met most of the guests here tonight. They were all the same.

Except for his hostess. Daniel turned to her and smiled, bowing a bit, showing he knew how to present a decent leg. Jane was his cousin, and a brighter, kinder soul he could never hope to meet. Married up, she had, and Daniel was sorry to see it, for all that he liked Gerard. The man was decent enough, but he moved in what passed for high society circles in their tiny parish, and Jane simply wasn't cruel enough for these people. A fox among the hounds, as it were.

The grateful look little Jane turned on him upon his arrival told him she was well into the desperate stage, and he immediately offered his arm to her, taking her for a turn about the room. Fair to be certain that no one would bother her when she was with him. Daniel was big enough and work hardened enough to be intimidating to these soft, bored people, and he exploited that advantage at every opportunity. Not to mention that most of these fops wouldn't be able to keep up with his stride.

"You look a bit frazzled, cousin," Daniel murmured.

"I am, I fear," Jane replied in her quiet voice. "The party seems to be going well, but I tire quickly these days, and everyone is so very clever. It is difficult for me to keep up."

"Gerard should know better than to ask you to host these damnable things in your confinement." A woman as far along in child bearing as Jane needed rest and quiet, not a flock of bright, sharp birds.

"Don't be unkind, Daniel. He has a position to maintain. And don't glower so at me. I am the one person in this room you cannot intimidate."

Conceding with a sigh, Daniel led Jane to the refreshment table for a glass of punch. They had been quite studiously ignoring the other guests in an attempt to give Jane much needed breathing room, and so were quite blindsided by the approach of a garishly dressed female with a heavily made-up face.

"Jane! Darling. You must introduce me to your friend."

Good lord. She had a voice like a chicken whose chicks were being eaten by a blacksnake. Daniel surmised that the lady, to use the term loosely, must be Madeline Barstow, newly arrived in the county. He had met her husband the previous day at the livestock auction, and he saw that the two were very well-matched indeed. Jane simply smiled politely and performed the introductions.

"Mrs. Henry Barstow, may I present my dear cousin, Daniel Calhoun. Daniel, Madeline Barstow, lately of Richmond."

"Madame," Daniel greeted, with the barest of nods.

"How delightful to meet some of Jane's family." The woman leaned forward, batting her sooty eyelashes and giving him a horrifying view of her shrunken cleavage. "Will you be here for the dancing later on this evening? I should very much like to see what sort of figure you present."

Blinking at the audacity of her double entendre, Daniel shook his head. "I'm not certain I shall. I have a mare in foal that I may be called away to deliver."

"How...capable."

Daniel tried very hard not to laugh aloud at her expression, and though Jane's face did not change, he could feel the stifled laughter in her chest where it pressed against his arm.

"Madeline does not care to get her hands dirty, I'm afraid." The new voice was deep, clipped, and offensive in tone. The man it belonged to was obviously just as offensive to judge from his expression, which was perhaps best summed up as ironic. Obviously a dandy, in his rich burgundy brocade, shot through with gold threads. His hair was simply done, though, and Daniel thought it was vanity rather than defiance that made him go un-powdered or without a wig. Unlike many of his peers, this man had a full head of hair, the color of burnished cherrywood. His eyes were brown, shot through with as bright a gold as his coat. And for all of his fancy looks and pale skin, he still managed to be completely masculine.

"Michael St. James, at your service. And may I echo Madeline and say what a pleasure it is to meet any of the fair Jane's relations?"

Prepared to bristle over any perceived insult of his cousin, Daniel frowned dampeningly at the man. But the smile St. James turned upon Jane was genuine, and for him, kind. The look he turned back upon Daniel, however, held a glint he could not decipher.

"At any rate," St. James said, "I do hope your mare holds off long enough for us all to learn a bit more about you, my good sir."

Daniel returned the fellow's insolent stare, squaring his shoulders, which made Madeline Barstow take a step back. Oh, how he wanted to laugh. Instead, Daniel settled for a curl of his lip and said, "Really. I cannot imagine why."

Michael was forced to hide a smile when the dainty elbow of Calhoun's cousin hit the man squarely in the ribs, drawing a grunt. The smile refused to remain hidden, however, when she frowned reprovingly at Daniel, and the man had the grace to look contrite.

"What he means," Jane said with a mild look, "is that he would be delighted to make your acquaintance, newly arrived as you are, Mr. St. James."

"Why, thank you Madame. And may I say that you are much more gracious and diplomatic than your cousin?"

"You may." Jane beamed at him, which transformed her rather handsome face into lovely.

The skin above Calhoun's ill-tied cravat turned a delightful shade of pink. As a beginning salvo, Michael could not have been more pleased. There was simply no need to treat Jane Gentry as if she were made of glass. The lady had a backbone of iron, for all of her delicate looks. And it was heartening to note that, while Daniel Calhoun obviously had teeth, he could be reined in when necessary. A superb amusement indeed.

"I hope I will also be able to feel that I know you better," Madeline said, and Michael was surprised to note that he had nearly forgotten the woman's presence.

Not swayed by his cousin's desire for social niceties in this instance, Calhoun raked the woman with a cool glance and replied, "I am sure you will be far too busy to come to know me very well, Mrs. Barstow. Doing good works for the church or some such. You will excuse us? I was just about to deliver

Jane to her husband."

They swept off, Jane offering Michael an apologetic look as she left. Madeline grabbed a glass of punch and gulped it down. "He has all the manners of a rooting pig."

"I was not aware that you chose your companions for their manners, Madeline."

"Well, he is glorious male animal, isn't he?" The speculation in Madeline's eyes made Michael a tad nauseated. She could no doubt afford her choice of companion, but he imagined those poor men must pay for their willingness to whore themselves.

Making a non-committal noise, Michael continued to eye the pair as they made their way across the room to Jane's husband, Gerard. A fine specimen, yes, a great draft horse of a man. Tall, imposing, and work-hardened, with large muscles that moved smoothly together under his best suit of clothes. A worthy mountain to climb, and Michael had every intention of reaching the summit long before someone like Madeline Barstow could sink in her pick.

"Really, Daniel, it's hardly like you to be quite so rude," Jane scolded.

"She deserved it." Daniel knew he sounded petulant, but he could not help it. These people drove him mad.

"Mrs. Barstow certainly did deserve it. She is

crude, and loose besides. I was speaking of Mr. St. James. He did little to merit your disapproval."

"You cannot be serious." Slanting a disbelieving glance at Jane, Daniel continued. "He's the worst sort of wastrel, you can tell that just by looking at his hands. Never done a decent day's work in his life. I found him most offensive."

"Well, he has been nothing but kind to me, as unpopular as I am, and seems to have no worries about toadying favor with anyone. For that alone I would like him. He seems lonely, though, doesn't he, displaced as he is? Perhaps someone should take him into confidence, befriend him." Her eyes took on the glow of missionary joy, as if she was giving alms to the poor. He'd seen that look many times, and it boded ill for the person Jane chose to take on her little projects.

"Oh, no. No, indeed. You will not drag me down with another of your charity cases. And let me assure you, someone like Michael St. James can find friends wherever he goes. He needs no help from me. Ah, Gerard. Please deflect your wife from trying to force me into kindly social deeds."

The gentleman in question, Gerard Gentry, was a slightly balding man with soft blue eyes and a gentle, continuously befuddled expression. Blinking, he shook his head at Daniel and offered Jane his arm. "Far be it from me to stop her once she puts her mind to something." He patted Jane's hand. "Darling, are you all right? You look pale."

"I should like to sit down, I think."

"Certainly. Certainly, dear. I told you this would be too much for you."

Thank goodness he was not on the receiving end of that look, Daniel thought. And he should have known the party was Jane's idea, rather than Gerard's for all that he had blamed it on the man. Jane was very protective of her husband, not wanting to hold him back through her presence in his life, and therefore did things she should not, just to keep up appearances. In turn, Gerard was a loving husband, who tried his best to convince Jane that he neither cared about nor needed society as long as he had her. For that, Daniel admired him enormously. The constant skullduggery between them, however, made him want to bash their heads together.

"I was just telling Daniel that he should befriend young Mr. St. James, Gerard. Don't you think so?"

"Oh, yes, that would be smashing." Gerard's face lit up. "He needs a few friends here, I believe, to keep him from falling in with someone like that dreadful Barstow woman. I understand he likes horses. You could take him to the auction, Saturday next. That would be perfectly marvelous."

"I really don't think—"

"Why don't you get him, Gerard dear, and bring him over so Daniel can ask him?" Jane's face lit up with her zeal.

Ever dutiful, Gerard pattered off, smiling

happily. "You," Daniel said, "are diabolical. I have no intention of asking that blasted man to go anywhere with me."

"I think it would be good for you. You have an unreasoning prejudice against anyone who does not farm, Daniel. It is time you broadened your horizons."

"Bullshit."

"Daniel!"

"I beg your pardon Jane, but confound it, I do not want to get to know the man, and I have work to do on Saturday next."

"Well then, you shall have to explain to him why you cannot take him to the auction." Jane gestured across the room, where Gerard was tugging a bemused looking St. James towards them. "I'm sure Gerard has already made the offer."

"I will repay you for this, Jane. In full. I assure you."

It proved exceptionally difficult to remain straight-faced as Gerard dragged him across the room toward Jane and Daniel Calhoun. Gerard explained that Daniel wished to show him about the county, a deed best accomplished by accompanying him to the stock auction Saturday next, since they both had a fondness for horses. Now who, he wondered, had brought about that brilliant idea?

From the thunderous look on Calhoun's face, and the serene smile on Jane's, Michael thought he could lay it squarely at the lady's door. He had a distinct urge to kiss the toes of her dainty slippers.

This could not be more perfect had he planned it himself. In fact, this was better, for he'd had no hand in it, and could therefore pretend disingenuousness. Ever since their initial encounter earlier in the evening Michael had been casting about for a reasonable way to spend time with delectable Daniel Calhoun, and now he had one, presented on a silver platter and covered in brandy sauce.

"Here he is, darling," Gerard said proudly, and it struck Michael that the man was thoroughly domesticated. It would be horrifying if the two were not so obviously in love and so genuinely deserving of kindness.

Bowing, Michael inquired, "You wished to speak with me, Madame?"

With a light tap of Daniel's arm with her fan, Jane replied, "Actually, Daniel wished to ask you something. Didn't you, cousin?"

"Certainly. Jane insists that I take you to the local pony sale. I suppose you will agree and therefore bind me to a day of insufferable boredom?" Calhoun's eyes flashed with irritation, his mouth set in a hard line.

Both Jane and Gerard gasped at Daniel's rudeness, but Michael answered before either of them scolded him. "Of a certainty. For you see, that will save me from a day of boredom myself. A day spent annoying you will make my life far richer."

"Oh, I say, well done!" That from Gerard, and Michael got the feeling the man was happy to see Daniel answered in kind for a change. Jane reinforced the opinion when she laughed, a truly lovely sound, and smacked Daniel on the shoulder.

"There," she said, "I think you have met your match, Daniel Calhoun. Someone you cannot frighten away, and who will show you wit for wit."

"I thought that was you, my dear," Daniel said gallantly, then turned a sour frown on Michael. "I suppose if I must, I must. You may come to my home by precisely eight o'clock in the morning on Saturday next if you wish to accompany me. I will not wait for you. I must hope that you are satisfied, Jane. And I fear that I have overstayed my limit insofar as my patience is concerned. I shall return for the dancing, but for now I believe I will have a smoke."

With a kiss on Jane's cheek, and another admirable glower at Michael, Daniel took his leave. Jane turned to Michael, ready to apologize, but he forestalled her with a raised hand.

"Do not excuse him, my dear lady. There is really no need. It's refreshing to meet someone who speaks his mind in that manner. I very much look forward to furthering our acquaintance."

Clearly relieved, Jane smiled brightly at him.

Gerard simply looked amazed. "I say," he said. "You are far more tolerant than I. Jane's cousin is a fine man, but I find his manner difficult in the extreme."

Watching Daniel's retreating back disappear out the side door of the ballroom, Michael simply shook his head. "If there's one thing I find challenging, sir, it is difficult people. I am one myself, you see, and so have a great affinity for them."

Rolling his shoulders, Daniel looked down the road at the big bay horse clattering toward him. His eyes were full of the grit that lack of sleep produced, but even so he could see Michael St. James was nothing if not prompt. Damnation. Daniel had so hoped the man would sleep in late enough to miss their little excursion.

After the invitation was issued at the soiree by his cousin Jane, Daniel had studiously avoided Michael St, James. It was fully his intention that St. James understood that, while Daniel felt an obligation to stand behind his family's promises, he did not like it. The few times he had seen the man about town since then, St. James had seemed amused rather than affronted, and Daniel wondered what in the name of all holy things it took to offend him. He would do his utmost to find out.

Especially today. He had a feeling it was

precisely eight o'clock. It was indeed Saturday. And sadly, Daniel was the one unprepared to leave on time. Dispassionately, Daniel decided that St. James did at least have good taste in horses. The bay, obviously a gelding, had excellent conformation. Deep chest. Well balanced legs. Smooth gait. He was still an annoying bastard, however.

"Good morning, Calhoun," the man called out, reining in his mount and looking Daniel over intently. "It would appear you are not dressed for town."

"It would appear so. You are welcome to go on without me, if you wish. Or you may wait while I wash up and change into more suitable attire."

"I shall wait. What would your dear cousin Jane say if she heard I attended the sale alone? She would be most disappointed, I vow."

"Yes. At least until she heard that one of my mares was down with the colic all night."

Immediately, St. James dismounted, a concerned look settling on his features. "Did she pull through? Is there aught I can do to help?"

Looking over the man's fine feathers dubiously, Daniel shook his head. "She's on the road to recovery, I'm glad to say. I've left a groom with her to keep her up and walking. Besides, it wouldn't do for you to soil your frippery."

Cocking his head to one side, St. James looked at Daniel in amused inquiry. "You, sir, seem to have taken an instant dislike to me. I wonder why."
20

"I dislike people who hide a lack of substance behind fine clothes and finer words," Daniel snapped.

"And you feel I am one of those people?"

"I do, sir."

Rather than become angry, the irritating fellow simply laughed. It was a surprisingly genuine sound. "Then I shall have to convince you of my worth. And it is refreshing to find someone not blinded by my charms. If you wish, Mr. Calhoun, we could skip the auction for this day and you may simply show me about your property. That would satisfy your cousin, and keep you from having to go into town when you are so obviously not disposed to do so. I know that despite her apparent recovery, colic is worrisome, and you want to stay close to the mare, as well. Does that sound like a fair option?"

Daniel narrowed his eyes at the man, instantly suspicious. "More than fair. Which is why I must find your motives a bit suspect, St. James."

It was not often that someone could chide him for his lack of social niceties and make him sorry for it. Daniel was not precisely sorry for it now, but he felt his ears and cheeks go hot, like he was a schoolboy being reprimanded for forgetting his hornbook. The very calm, reasonable tone of St. James' voice as he cataloged Daniel's offenses made him feel very petty indeed. Motioning for the man to follow him, Daniel led the way into the stable, calling out to a groom to fetch the tack they'd left behind.

Damn the man, St. James discomfited Daniel more than anyone had in years. Look at him, Daniel thought, in his superbly tailored buff breeches and shined-to-perfection boots. A man of that ilk shouldn't be able to unsaddle a mount with the economy of motion this one had shown. Nor should he be able to bandy words about in such an intelligent manner. Once you dug a bit deeper than the surface, St. James' sort of dandy usually turned out to be nothing more than a good mimic, aping the jibes of his more cerebral peers. Not so with this one, and Daniel was, in a word, annoyed. He would much prefer the man fit into his neatly made slot in Daniel's head.

"You may stable him here, St. James," Daniel said, indicating a freshly cleaned stall. "I shall have my groom give him a rubdown, and some water and oats. Unless he is on special feed?"

"Oats will be fine. And I thank you. May I also thank you to call me Michael? St. James makes me feel as if I should be done up in stained glass, hanging on a cathedral wall."

"I fear not," Daniel replied. "For then I should be obliged to ask you to call me Daniel, and I have no wish for us to become intimates."

Again that deep, hearty laugh which sounded so genuine and was almost infectious. Almost. Daniel fought a smile, and St. James shook his head. "You are the stubbornest fellow I have met in an age, barring my father. And there's no need for you to become intimate with me to call me by my given name, Calhoun. Although given time, I might change your mind about that too."

Something in the undertone of the man's words made Daniel shift from one foot to another uncomfortably. Perhaps it was the difference in emphasis on the word they had both used. Perhaps it was the slow sweep of St. James' gaze over his face and form. Whatever the reason, Daniel felt it prudent to retreat. "I'll just get the groom," he said. "And if you feel it necessary, I shall call you Michael. But you may call me Calhoun," Daniel finished.

"Fair enough."

God in Heaven, it was indecent for a man who was exhausted and filthy to look so utterly edible. Saying that Daniel Calhoun was not dressed for a trip into town was an understatement. He was dressed for very little that involved polite company. Buckskin breeches worn almost obscenely thin hugged the man's strong thighs and hung precariously from his hipbones. They were obviously once good riding trousers. Now they were for work, and they fit well enough to give Michael a tantalizing picture of what lay beneath them. High boots, suitable for mucking about in the stables, fit tightly along muscled calves and highlighted the extraordinary length of Daniel's legs. The most devastating thing, however, was that Daniel was shirtless. The rough linen shirt he had been wearing was draped over the hitching post beside the barn, where it had obviously been left so Daniel could scrub off in the horse trough.

Faced with the expanse of flesh that bared chest presented, Michael was amazed that he could form coherent words, let alone engage in witty repartee, so he was rather pleased with himself. Smooth, golden skin, layered over firm muscles obviously gained from physical labor. Not enough fur to be off putting. Just enough, in fact, sprinkled from nipple to nipple and descending in a decidedly intriguing trail to the waistband of those positively amazing breeches. The spring morning was brisk, and Michael was certain the trough water was cold, which would account for the hardness of the man's nipples. An altogether pleasing picture he was in no hurry to alter, hence the suggestion that they stay on Daniel's farm for the day.

Not that Michael was entirely selfish in his thinking. A horse that went down with colic was still in danger during the recovery period, and Michael was certain Calhoun would prefer to be nearby. Not that he would belabor thenotion by repeating it. Far be it from him to disabuse the man of his base assumptions. No, indeed. In fact, he intended to play them for all he was worth. Now, where was he? Oh, yes.

Daniel went about finding a groom, and Michael set about taking the saddle and pads off his horse. When Daniel came back, he got a quizzical look from the man.

"You're quite good with him. Why are you really doing this?" Daniel asked.

Again, the blunt force of the question had Michael smiling.

"My motives are most benign, sir. You will find I am simply bored. Bucolic gentility does not suit me. Unfortunately, I have no choice but to be here in the country. So I am but amusing myself. Still, there is no reason for my amusement to afford you any more inconvenience than it already has. I am not prepared to apologize for forcing my company upon you," Michael finished with a smile. "But I am willing to allow that you have obligations to your household which will force a change of plans."

"How magnanimous of you."

"Oh, indeed I am. I rode all the way out here, and now you've made me care for my own horse, despite your offer of a groom. I think I shall stay through luncheon, at least. I trust you will let me have some bread and water, or whatever else you feed unwanted interlopers of no substance. Lead the way, sir."

The tips of Calhoun's ears turned red again, and Michael had the feeling it was embarrassment rather than anger. And so it should be. The man was deliberately insulting, and while it amused him to no end, Michael had no intention of letting it go unremarked. He would give as good as he got.

"Oh, very well. Come along and I will show you the barns. And yes, I will feed you. Jane will no doubt have my balls if I do not and she hears of it. Beware, though, I may put you to even more work than unsaddling your horse."

Calhoun was proving to be as entertaining as he was attractive. So certain was he of Michael's character on such short acquaintance. It appeared he did not like to have his convictions shaken, either, for the man was clearly flustered. Really, did he think making Michael call him Calhoun would keep them at a safe distance? Hardly. Nor would making him muck out stalls, should it come to that.

"So, Calhoun, has your family always owned this land, or is this your own acquisition?"

Another sideways suspicious look came his way, as if Daniel was deciding if Michael was mocking him. He met the look with a politely curious one of his own, bland as milk. It pleased Michael when Daniel decided to trust and began explaining the mechanics of his working farm. As he expounded on how the land had been his father's, but all of the improvements including house and stable were from his own planning and labor, Michael found that he was actually impressed. The effort it must have cost Daniel to create and maintain such a concern was admirable, if not completely understandable. There was also the added bonus that discussing something he so obviously loved caused the sour expression to melt from Daniel's face, where it was replaced by a sincere, quiet joy.

Which meant, of course, that it was time to stick a pin in the bladder and let out the air. "You seem very content to play gentleman farmer, Calhoun."

Precisely as he expected, Daniel wheeled on him, a formidable scowl forming on his face. "I play at nothing, sir. I am not a dilettante, as some people are, happy to do nothing of value. This farm produces crops, which feed not only my workers, house staff, and immediate family but also that of my father's house, since he cannot be bothered to do any sort of labor. Much like yourself, he prefers leisure. I also provide my dear cousin Jane with the foodstuff she serves at those fancy dress balls you so enjoy. I hope you will do me the favor from now on of keeping your opinion of my livelihood to yourself."

Righteous indignation suited Daniel almost as well as the smile it had replaced. "Why should I, I wonder? You've certainly seen fit to belittle me at every occasion. I will admit my choice of words was poor, however. I meant no disrespect. In fact, I admire your work ethic."

"As you have none of your own."

"So it would seem. Aren't you chilled?"

The abrupt change of subject had the desired affect. Indignation gave way before confusion. "I beg your pardon?"

"Prancing about half naked like that. I would think it a bit too early in the spring to go the way of the unclothed savage."

Understanding dawned on Calhoun's face, and he crossed his arms over his bare chest. "You," Daniel said with a completely serious look, "are quite possibly the most offensive man I have ever met."

Modestly studying his nails to hide an impudent grin, Michael replied, "Considering you keep your own company so much, that must be quite a feat."

Daniel stared, arms crossed, utterly self-conscious now that St. James had pointed out his lack of attire. Damn the man. Damn, damn, damn. He did not want to give St. James a tour. Nor did he want to feed the man luncheon. Or listen to him snipe. And Daniel certainly did not want to give the man a show, for there was something in the way St. James looked at his bare chest that reminded him of the way he might look at a woman in her corselet.

Which was ridiculous, no doubt. The tour of the barn took him by Fatima's stall, however, where a tunic hung that he used for shoeing, and Daniel pulled it on, trying not to look completely obvious, knowing he failed when Michael's mouth twisted in a dark smile.

Bastard.

"Oh, who is this sweet lady?" St James no longer looked at him; instead, he leaned on Fatima's stall and peered at her, looking utterly entranced. It made the pit of his belly feel odd, that look, and the feeling made him angry by turn so he snapped.

"She is far too valuable for you to be playing about. Come away from there."

"Oh, dear me. I apologize abjectly for infecting her with my presence."

The words came accompanied by a raised brow and a look so offensive that Daniel found his fists balling up in an attempt not to strike the man down. No one had ever piqued his temper so, and that was saying a great deal. His temper was the stuff of legend in the county.

As if he knew what Daniel struggled with, St. James moved close, titling his chin up as if to say, "Try it".

Daniel backed up one step, then two. "I simply meant she is high strung and might bite or kick, and injure either you or herself."

"Ah. She is much like her owner, then."

"Yes. I would beware that." Daniel bared his teeth. Damn the man. Goodness, he did not think he had ever spent so much time damning one particular person.

"Oh, I find it adds spice. Shall we continue?" Michael asked.

"Yes." Daniel straightened his spine, determined

not to let this infuriating man get the better of him. "This is my best breeding stock…"

The tour went on and on, Daniel waxing enthusiastic about his lands and his horses, and he scarce noticed Michael was actually listening, indeed, was quite polite and interested. Only when one of his bondsmen announced that his luncheon was prepared did Daniel realize they had spent some four hours in company and had not murdered one another.

How amazing.

"Well," he said grudgingly. "I suppose you will have your luncheon after all."

"Excellent. Where may I wash up?"

Daniel led the way to his home, immediately foisting Michael off on a servant to bathe his hands and face, giving Daniel the opportunity to call for a clean shirt and to gain some equilibrium. He was not meant to like Michael St. James. No indeed. The man could converse intelligently about horses, certainly. That did not make him any less of a ne'er do well.

Surely not.

Once properly dressed against St. James' unnerving eyes, Daniel ascended to find the man himself waiting, looking as casually elegant as ever, as if he had not spent the entire morning tromping about a working farm. It was most annoying.

Luncheon was a brief affair, a cold collation with breads and early fruits and smoked meats. If Daniel expected complaint he was sorely disappointed, for Michael ate heartily and bade him praise his cook.

"I assure you that took little effort."

One of Michael's infuriatingly agile eyebrows rose. "I assure you all endeavors in the kitchen take effort. One should always praise the cook, just as one should always tip the laundress."

Now he was being chided for his treatment of servants! Daniel felt his face heat once more. So much for their pleasant truce. Michael seemed even more determined than he to undermine it.

"You are quite the most deliberately offensive man I have ever met. Do you never let sleeping dogs lie?"

"You are far from sleepy, my dear Calhoun. You are a dog with bite, and I find you endlessly fascinating."

"Yes, well." Daniel blustered, feeling not so much fascinating as foolish. "I think perhaps you should go now."

"I suppose I ought. I have no doubt overstayed my welcome. But you must let me return the favor and come to luncheon at my home next week."

To be faced with this man on his home ground? Daniel thought not. "Thank you, no. I am sure I shall be busy."

"Nonsense. That is what you have a staff for. If you do not agree, I shall be heartbroken and shall be forced to go to your cousin to bare my soul and inform her of my stricken state."

He stared. St. James stared back, whiskey eyes wide and guileless, utterly unbelievable. Daniel fingered the edge of the pristine white linen of his table runner and thought hard, trying to find a way out.

Sadly, he could not, not if he did not wish Jane to be involved, for Michael would surely follow through on his threat.

"You are despicable," Daniel grated out.

"Thoroughly."

The man simply would not be insulted.

"I will see you at ten o'clock then. Saturday next." Michael waited, an expectant smile on his face. It made Daniel wish to hit him again. No doubt someday he would.

"I said I would be there, and so I will. Now, please take yourself off. A groom will assist you with your mount."

Laughing, St. James stood, giving him a courtly bow once afoot. "Thank you for the most entertaining day I have had since I adjourned to this Godforsaken backwater, Calhoun. I look forward to our next meeting."

With that, St. James left him, and Daniel could not help stare at the man's rather shapely backside as he went. Whatever was the matter with him?

He would not look forward to seeing St. James again. Not one bit.

Chapter Two

The day of his visit to Michael's home dawned sunny and beautiful, naturally. The world was greening, the trees and grasses Daniel loved so much turning out with the reckless abandon, flowers popping up at the sides of the road. Would that he were in the mood to enjoy it. No, instead he must travel to subject himself to the most infuriating, obnoxious fellow he had ever laid eyes on.

His legs must have communicated his tension to his mount, for Ibrahim danced beneath him, snorting and tossing. Daniel patted the big dapple gelding's neck, letting go of as much of his ire as he could. There was no sense in making them both miserable.

In fact, when Ibrahim sidestepped again, Daniel decided he knew how to make them both happy. He would give the gelding his head and let him run. He could not be far from Michael's home now, and the road was as deserted as he had ever seen it.

Kicking lightly, Daniel let Ibrahim have the bit,

and they were off, the big gelding clattering off at full speed. Utterly exhilarating, the wind whistling past his ears, the feel of a heavily muscled beast moving beneath him in perfect time, the blur of the scenery.

Ibrahim ran and ran until they finally crested a small rise and St. James' new residence came into view. Daniel kicked Ibrahim into an even faster run, ending at the carriage return in front of St. James' home, just in time to throw divots of dirt at the man's feet as he stepped out of his door.

"Well," St. James said, one dark eyebrow rising. "You certainly know how to make an entrance, Calhoun."

Feeling defiant and a bit self-righteous after being dragged into this luncheon, Daniel simply nodded, letting Ibrahim dance entirely too close to the man. St. James did not move save to pat the gelding's steaming neck.

"I have called up a groom. I, at least, will not make you walk him out yourself."

"Oh, ho, I am duly chastised, St. James." Daniel swung down to the ground, pulling off his gloves, then scratching Ibrahim's ears in praise. "I am, however, unimpressed by it."

"Certainly you are."

A young groom came and smiled shyly at him, taking Ibrahim's bridle with authority and leading the horse away. Daniel sighed, as it had been helpful to have the big gray between himself and Michael as a buffer.

He mounted the stairs, ignoring Michael's outstretched hand. "Well, I suppose there must be a tour. I believe I have been to this property before. Master Byrd once owned it, did he not?"

"He did, as you well know. Jane informs me you once both played here as children. However, if you would like to see the improvements I have made, you are welcome. I have not been here long, but I admit, I took it upon myself to spruce things up."

He could easily see the improvements. The stairs themselves were white once more, the marble washed until it gleamed. The columns and façade of the neo-classical building were sparkling clean. The neatly trimmed hedgerows and greening gave every indication Michael took as much care with his home as he did with his own appearance, and it surprised Daniel greatly.

"Do come in, Calhoun. See the inside."

Daniel trailed after St. James, noting the silk stockings, the gray superfine trousers, and the dark blue coat. Really, the man cut a fine portrait, one that had Daniel scowling at the back of the fine head of dark reddish-brown hair.

The interior of the house impressed equally, the smoke-stained walls now white washed, the candle lamp that had once dripped wax upon the foyer floor replaced with a chandelier with dangles and baubles and wax catchers.

"How extravagant."

"A gift from my mother. She felt I needed

a modicum of civilization, at least. Shall we? I thought we might play chess before luncheon. If you play?"

"You have a mother?"

St. James turned laughing eyes on him. "Well, I came into the world the usual way, Calhoun. So yes."

Snorting, Daniel shook his head. "One assumes you hatched, St. James. Like an exotic bird. Or perhaps sprang from Jove's head like Minerva."

Michael laughed harder, the sound deep and true. "How very flattering. You delight me, Daniel. Come, I will arrange for us to have cider. Elias!"

Elias turned out to be a valet-cum-footman of indeterminate age who brought them cider and cakes. The easy manner between master and servant rather surprised him, for he expected such a man as St. James to be imperious and unkind, rather than jocular and relaxed. Michael constantly amazed him. Daniel liked it not at all, for he preferred to know what lay underfoot.

The chessboard sat laid out in a handsomely appointed study. Grand French high-backed chairs made substantial seating, unlike the tiny bergere chairs favored by most of their neighbors. The chairs were done in mahogany, with a jacquard fabric, and Daniel was struck not so much by their quality as by the signs of use they showed. A popinjay should not have shabby furniture.

"You surprise me, St. James. Your furniture is

most out of fashion, according to my cousin Jane, at least."

"I have a parlor full of fashionably tiny furniture should anyone save you come to visit me, pariah that I am. You need not worry. Shall we play?"

Those eyes teased him, mocked him. Daniel nodded sharply, gesturing. "I shall even let you go first, as I intend to make short work of you."

"We shall see about that."

Indeed, Michael played with far more skill than he expected, making him scramble to keep up. The challenge actually warmed him, and Daniel bent to it with enthusiasm, his victory making him want to crow. He smiled over at Michael, feeling better about this assignation than he had since he agreed to come.

"Well played, St. James."

"Indeed. You are quite the tactician. Ah, I see luncheon is prepared."

Elias hovered behind his shoulder, Daniel discovered, discreetly waiting for them to finish. Daniel nodded, stood. "This has worked up quite an appetite."

"Oh, my, yes."

The glint in Michael's eyes unsettled him, made Daniel stand and follow Elias as quickly as he could, ignoring the tingle Michael's gaze engendered. Surely he had no reason to *tingle* over the man. Really!

They sat down to eat in the morning room, as

the formal dining room was apparently another of those showrooms Michael had in the event of guests, and the chairs, St. James said, would give way under his magnificent frame.

Magnificent.

Daniel scowled as he felt his cheeks heat.

"Really, St. James, it makes me wonder, the notice you take of my frame."

"And so it should."

With a smile that explained no more than his words, St. James bade him eat. While the meal was much more elaborate than the cold collation he had served Michael, it was still simple and hearty, not at all the flight of continental fancy he had expected.

He sat back when he finished the last morsel, utterly replete. "I say, St. James. My compliments to the cook."

"I shall tell her. Or rather, Elias will. Should we take some exercise?"

"I believe so." His rounded belly told him he ought, or he would be falling asleep in no time, and he had chores to accomplish upon his return home. A bit of a walk would settle things, and move his humors about, as well.

They took a turn out in the yard, ending at the stable. St. James did not posses the sort of breeding stock Daniel did, but he did have that fine stallion, and a few well-turned geldings, deep in chest, long in leg.

"Good stock."

"Yes. It is."

St. James was close behind him, so close Daniel could feel the man's breath on his neck. Whirling about, Daniel met Michael's eyes, close enough that every lash could be distinguished, andDaniel could see the flecks of gold that made Michael's brown eyes seem amber.

"What in blazes are you doing?" Daniel asked, trying to back up, but finding his back to a wall.

"Something I will no doubt regret. But I must."

It was the most foolhardy and extraordinary thing anyone had ever done to him; Michael went up on tiptoe and kissed his mouth. Stunned, Daniel let him, his mouth falling open with utter shock, a disbelieving noise tearing from him. Evidently Michael took that as an invitation and pressed with his tongue between Daniel's lips, running it around the tender insides.

Immediately Daniel pushed St. James away, his fist crashing just under the man's left eye. Michael went down as if a felled tree, legs straight and back unbent, measuring his length in the dust as Daniel stood over him, fists clenched.

"How dare you! You filthy bounder! I vow, I should call you out."

"But you will not." Sitting up, St. James rubbed blood from his lips, grinning up at Daniel wildly.

"Why not, I ask you?"

Those whiskey eyes trailed down his body, stopping at level with his groin. "Because you liked it."

His lower body had indeed betrayed him, his cock rising to press against the placket of his trousers. Unable to speak for his fury—and, yes, his fear—Daniel turned on his heel and left, saddling his horse and riding out as if the hounds of Hell were upon his heels.

Or perhaps the devil in the form of Michael St. James.

Chapter Three

Michael sat in his study, composing a letter to his mother. His dressing gown shielded him from the worst of the late spring breezes, and thoughts of Daniel Calhoun kept him quite warm enough, thank you, despite the large bruise he sported on his face.

Good God, the man had spirit! Michael loved it, adored a man who would not be trampled. He also liked the way Daniel tasted, and he was most determined to taste again, and very soon at that.

Until then, he would simply have to depend upon his imagination, which was admittedly well developed. He looked at the piece of foolscap his letter occupied and let out a surprised curse. He had left a large smear of ink on the page, obliterating a good fourth of the text. Damnation. It had taken him the better part of an hour to write something that was not a single, long, inflammatory complaint on the situation he found himself in. Now it was ruined.

Sighing, Michael went to pour himself a drink,

going not to his desk with brandy in hand but to his most comfortable chair. He sat, head back and eyes closed, thinking about the last day's work.

He had probably alienated Daniel Calhoun to the point of no return, but really, how could he have resisted? The man was a delight. The brandy stung his torn lip, and Michael smiled. Damn, but Calhoun had been perfectly magnificent in his rage. Fierce. Frightened half to death judging from the way he'd turned tail and ran.

His cock stirred under the heavy brocade of his dressing gown, and Michael let his legs fall open, the hand not holding the snifter coming to rub at the stiff ridge of his shaft. Oh, the things he could teach Daniel Calhoun! What would it be like to touch that large, muscled form, to see Daniel in his pleasure? He had no doubt that deep passions raged inside Daniel Calhoun, and those passions would spill out given the right provocation.

That might even make his exile worthwhile.

Setting the brandy aside on a small inlaid wood table, Michael began to touch himself in earnest, opening his gown and sliding his hand inside to wrap about his shaft and pull. He did not take his time; this was no leisurely fantasy. He needed badly.

Instead, he stroked himself fully, from base to head, thumb working the looser skin at the tip. Thoughts of how Calhoun would smell, how he would sound, filled Michael's head, urging him on, and his sac drew up tight against the base of his shaft, sending pure pleasure up his spine.

With a low cry, Michael spilled into his hand, sitting there for some time afterward, waiting for his breathing to slow.

Yes. He would have Daniel Calhoun, he decided. No matter the amount of effort involved. He was not one to turn away from a challenge, especially when the result was something he desired this badly.

No matter the cost.

Daniel avoided Michael St. James for a good, long while. Months, in fact, which was not an easy thing in the small county they lived in. Sadly, it was not so easy to avoid hearing about the man.

"I say, did you know that St. James fellow won the local derby? Not at all like you to miss it, Daniel."

That from Master Byrd, who was quite the only famous name in their parish. From Mrs. Heatherington he heard, "He even came to church the other day. Why, Daniel, he is simply *charming*."

Everywhere he went he heard about that blasted St. James, whether good or ill. It made his teeth grind. Really, what was it about the man that fascinated people so?

Indeed, what was it about the man that fascinated *him* so?

After their last meeting, Daniel was certain he never wanted to see the fellow again. What sort of a man kissed another man in such a way? Surely not a natural one. The assertion that Daniel, too, had enjoyed it was an absurd one. It had surprised him. Shocked him into immobility for a short time. But he had not enjoyed it, no matter what his cock wanted him to think.

The fact that he had gone to visit Sally the tavern wench at the Owl immediately afterward was purely coincidental.

At any rate, Daniel had managed to avoid St. James at the derby, at church, and at the weekly horse auction, and that was all fine and well with him. Which was why he stared at Jane as if she had grown another head when she insisted he invite Michael to the party he was hosting in honor of her new child, a baby boy named Daniel Gerard.

"Are you mad, cousin? I refuse."

He was at Jane's home, perched upon one of the ridiculously small chairs in her morning room. The birth had taken a great deal out of her, and she only now began to look herself, the pale, pinched expression of pain she'd worn for weeks finally receding. Which was, of course, why he did not roar at her. He simply, adamantly, refused.

"Daniel! How unkind. You said this was to be my soiree."

"It is to be held in my home, Jane. I gave you that much. Do not push. I will not have him about."

Her lower lip began to stick out in a most worrisome way. Daniel had great difficulty resisting that lower lip when used judiciously.

"He is kind to me."

It was said matter-of-factly, and without a hint of self-pity, but it made Daniel flinch. Many people were unkind to Jane in their parish, and while most everyone invited to the party would attend, as Daniel rarely hosted such events, most people would not be there to see Jane.

Damnation. Daniel hated being backed into a corner, but Jane had done it neatly without any real effort. Daniel would not hurt her for the world.

If it was St. James that Jane required, it was he she would get.

"Very well," he said with ill grace. "But do not be disappointed if he does not attend." Which he might not, Daniel thought, given the split lip Daniel had left him with on their last run in.

"Oh, I feel certain he will." Jane's dark eyes, so like his, glowed with pleasure and she rose to come and kiss his cheek. "Thank you, darling cousin."

Daniel harrumphed. "Do not thank me yet, dear Jane. We must both still survive this damnable party."

"I feel certain we are up to the task."

He gave her a dark look, knowing it would be an almost insurmountable task. "I hope you're right."

The invitation came almost too late. It arrived the afternoon the soiree was to be held, and if Michael St. James were a less suspicious man he would have thought it was a simple error of the post.

Instead he rather thought Daniel meant for it to arrive late. Still, he had time, and as it was clear from the invitation that the party was for Jane, whom he had not seen since she had produced Gerard's heir, well, how could he miss it?

"Elias!"

Elias was there immediately, and thank God for the man. He had been with Michael since early adulthood, was aware of his proclivities, and was discreet in all things. Wonderful man.

"I need my evening kit pressed, Elias. And my boots shined. You have precisely an hour."

"Yes, sir. Shall I have the carriage readied?"

"No, just my stallion. I need to get there rather quickly."

Elias just smiled and shook his head, "Yes, sir."

He would not be daunted by Daniel Calhoun's rudeness. This was a fine opportunity to pursue his goal of seducing Daniel, and to see Jane as well, whom he genuinely liked. She reminded him greatly of his mother, both for her kindness and her force of will.

He bathed with the water in his basin, and shaved his day's growth of beard before splashing on some bay rum. He dressed his hair simply, pulling it back into a smooth club at the back of is neck, and soon enough he was dressed in his formal evening wear, his stockings snowy white, his breeches of a deep, rich blue complementing the lighter silver and blue waistcoat and brocade cutaway frock coat. Yes, he thought as he placed his hat just so. He would do nicely.

Daniel's house looked entirely different in the early fall night than it did during a late spring day. The leaves on the large trees were just beginning to turn, and every window in the square façade was lit, making the place seem to glow. Charming.

He pulled up in front of Daniel's house and tossed his reins to a groom, one he remembered from before. "Take good care of him, lad."

"Yessir." The boy nodded, sketching him a tiny bow, and took his horse off. Time to face up to Mister Daniel Calhoun, and somehow Michael found he had flutters in his belly. How odd, if delightful all the same. Nerves had not beset him over a conquest since he'd reached adulthood and stopped the fumblings of youth.

Handing his invitation over to the footman at the door, who looked suspiciously like one of Jane Gentry's servants, Michael asked, "Is there a place I might refresh myself before going in? I had to ride here, you see."

"It is just like you to want to fluff your feathers before joining us, isn't it, St. James. The ladies' dressing room is just up the stairs and to the right."

Daniel strode into sight, color high on his cheeks.

"Ah, Calhoun. What a pleasure it is to see you again, too." Michael turned a syrupy smile on Daniel. "Thank you so much for inviting me, late though it was. Really, you almost managed your intent."

Ah, a direct hit. The flush he adored so rose above Daniel's collar, flooding into the man's cheeks. Mossy green eyes snapped their displeasure.

"If it were not for my cousin, St. James, you would not be here. It is still a grave temptation to have you feeling the weight of my fist again. I would *not* push, were I you."

"But you are not me." Giving up on refreshing his clothing, Michael handed his hat off as well as his coat and moved toward the doors to the formal drawing room. "Where is Jane? I should like to pay my respects."

As soon as they were out of earshot of the young footman, Daniel grabbed Michael's arm in a steely grip, surprising him into immobility. "You will be civil, St. James."

Michael gave Daniel a long, cool look. "My dear Calhoun," he said in his most offensive manner. "I have ever been civil, both to you and especially to Jane. She, at least, deserves my upmost respect. You are the one who insists upon being uncouth. Now unhand me."

To his everlasting surprise, Daniel did, the oddest look coming over the man's face. It might have been something akin to shame.

Dusting his coat sleeve, Michael went in search of Jane, when he truly whished to stay behind and needle Calhoun. Still, half of the battle was knowing when to stage a strategic retreat, and now was that time.

Jane looked quite well, smiling and chatting with a lady Michael had never met, much of the swelling she had exhibited in her last months of confinement having gone. Gerard had expressed worry about her health when Michael had seen him at auction, but she looked well recovered, and Michael was most pleased.

He walked over to her and presented a very creditable leg. "Jane. How good it is to see you out and about."

She took his hand, smiling up at him, and it struck him how pretty she was, really. He had never seen her when she had no discomfort associated with her childbearing, and she was lovely. "Michael. Wonderful. I feared you would not receive your invitation, though I browbeat Daniel into sending one. He can be so stubborn, you know."

"Oh, yes. I am well aware."

They shared a look of perfect understanding before Michael turned to Gerard, who was rather hovering. "Gentry. May I tell you how astonishingly lovely your wife is this evening?"

A flush of pride covered Gerard's cheeks, and he gave Jane a doting smile. "You may. Isn't she just stunning?"

"I think you have both fawned over her quite enough. Dance with me, Jane." Daniel shouldered past him and hauled Jane to her feet, making Gerard squawk and Michael laugh.

"Ever the gentleman, Calhoun," Michael chided.

"Yes? Well, what would you know about it, St. James?"

He heard Jane gasp, berating Daniel as they swept off, but it did not make him bat an eye. People about them might have, but Michael did not, not even when Gerard said, "I say, I don't think he likes you."

Michael watched Daniel tow Jane about the floor and grinned widely. "On the contrary. I think he's becoming quite fond."

"Daniel Calhoun. I am ashamed of you!" Jane's eyes snapped up at him, filled with true ire. Daniel sighed.

"I have reason."

"Do you indeed? Aside from your unreasoning prejudice against people who have wealth?" Jane asked.

"Yes." He growled the word, turning the heads of several other dancers. The country couple dance they engaged in was far too energetic to talk softly, so Daniel pulled Jane off to one side, getting them both a cup of punch before finding a private corner. "He's the worst sort, Jane."

"Why? Tell me why, Daniel, and I shall leave it alone."

Always so ready to believe in him, sweet Jane. She put a hand on his arm, looking at him earnestly. Waiting.

"He… I. Damnation, Jane. The man is a sodomite."

"Daniel!" Now she was the one drawing stares, and she lowered her voice with obvious effort, straight brows drawing down over her nose. "What a horrible thing to say."

"It is nothing but the truth. In fact, I was forced to lay the man out on our last meeting." Daniel would not allow himself to dwell on that kiss. No, he would not.

Her eyes widened. "What? Why?"

His cheeks heated almost painfully, and he looked away before answering, very quietly indeed. "He tried to kiss me."

"Really." Jane sat back with a thud, her own cheeks as pink as could be. She simply stared at him for the longest time. Then she cleared her throat delicately. "Was it pleasant?"

"Jane! Really, what a question. No it was not pleasant. I do not indulge in that sort of thing, and you know it."

She gave him a look that had the pure devil in it. "From what I understand, Daniel, you indulge in kissing a great deal. Molly down at the inn talks of you incessantly."

Good Gad. He did not wish to speak to Jane of his indiscretions. "How on earth do you know Molly? Such a lady you are."

"Yes, very much in the same vein as you are a gentleman. I grew up on a farm, just as you did, Daniel. It is the way of life. If you think I do not indulge, then how did I get with child?"

Daniel feared he would strangle on his own mortification if she kept talking. "Jane, please."

"Yes, yes. I apologize for offending your delicate sensibilities, but really Daniel, one kiss does not a sodomite make. He might very well have been trying to upset you. He seems to have a fiendish delight for your discomfort."

How could he explain to her the predatory gleam in Michael's eyes? Women were used to such things, he supposed, and did not notice them. They were not the hunters; they were the hunted. Daniel, however, was unaccustomed to the feeling.

He was saved from having to answer by the most unlikely of heroines—Mrs. Madeline Barstow. She came sweeping down upon them, bony torso left mostly bare by her fashionable new gown, which looked to Daniel to be more appropriate for sleeping or for the boudoir than for a country barn dance. The powdered hair was gone, as was the beauty mark, all of that claptrap obviously de trop now. She smiled at him with her painted lips, and it was truly terrifying.

"Jane, darling. Do you mind if I steal your

cousin away for a dance?"

"Well, Madeline, I do not. But you might ask Daniel if he minds."

'Twas all he could do not to laugh aloud. The look on the Barstow woman's face reminded him of nothing so much as a landed fish, mouth open, eyes bulging. Gads, it was good to see Jane back in rare form.

"I will have to beg off, Madame. My gout, you know."

He maintained a serious mien, though it was not easy with Jane shaking beside him, holding in her laughter. For the sake of the woman's remaining dignity, he did put a limp in his step as he took Jane back to Gerard. Humiliation was all well and good, but he didn't really need a new enemy.

"Did I invite her?" he asked, settling Jane with her delighted husband.

"No. She will arrive forthwith at any gathering, including a funeral of someone she does not know."

"Jane, how unkind." That was from Gerard, though he did not look as if he were terribly upset.

"How utterly true. I know you just got seated, dear lady, but may I have this dance?"

Daniel stiffened, shooting a dagger glare at Michael St. James. It was, of course, ignored, and Jane put her hand in Michael's, going back to the crush of bodies on the ballroom floor without so much as a glance his way.

"Oh, dear. You don't suppose he means to

seduce her, do you?" Gerard asked, fluttering like a portly dove.

He looked at Gerard in surprise, then shook his head wryly. "No, Gerard. I doubt he means any such thing. I don't think Jane is his sort at all."

"Are you really a sodomite?"

The question was asked with such sweet, patently false innocence that Michael tripped over his own feet, causing them to blunder through a few steps less than gracefully. Then he laughed heartily. What a delight Jane was, a smaller, gentler copy of her cousin. "And if I am? Will you tell the parish priest and have me run out of town?"

She considered that very seriously, brows drawn low. "Well, I cannot judge a man on anything but his actions, and you have been faultlessly kind to me, and wonderfully rude to Daniel, so I believe I must say no. Are you pursuing him?"

"Yes."

"I see." They jumped about vigorously for a moment or two, the intricate steps of the dance separating them. When they came back together, she smiled. "Very well. You have my blessing."

He stared. He could not help it.

Jane simply looked at him, very seriously. "If you ever hurt him, however, I will be forced to do great damage to you, do you understand?"

Michael nodded. She was a lioness with her cub. It was most amusing, and rather frightening. He liked her a great deal.

"Yes, my dear, Jane. I believe I do."

Chapter Four

The livestock auction bustled with life. The smell of horses and manure was strong; so was the smell of unwashed man, unfortunately. Daniel wrinkled his nose. Was it not for the fine stud he knew was to be up today, he would not have come. Truly, his mood was full of bile, and he did not wish to be among his so-called peers.

The mares all left him cold. This one was too short in the leg, that one not deep enough in the chest. Daniel waited impatiently for the uncut males, wanting to bid on the stallion and be away.

Sadly, he was forced to wait on the huge crop of geldings first.

Not a one of them was even the least bit interesting to him, not until the very last, a big bay the auctioneer called fractious. And hog feed. What truly caught his attention about the animal was the scarring on its hind end. Daniel loathed seeing any animal mistreated, and any man who would whip a horse so deserved to be whipped himself.

The opening bid was so low as to be ridiculous, and Daniel was just about to raise his paddle to make sure he outbid the few rough men who would buy such a cheap horse and work it to death when he heard a bid called out that was nearly quadruple the opening price.

The voice came clear and familiar, and Daniel looked for Michael St. James, assuming the man was trying to impress him. It soon became evident, however, that St. James had not even seen him. The man strode to the front of the bidding area, tapping his crop against his booted leg. Michael's expression dared the crowd of milling men to cross him, and none of them did, the auctioneer declaring him the winner of the sale.

How imperious he was. In this instance, Daniel admired it, as Michael took the lead of the gelding in hand, disdaining the stout grooms who offered to help him with the excitable nag. A few soft words had the animal becalmed enough to walk him out of the auction space, and Daniel turned to bidding on his stallion, the image of St. James stroking the gelding's scarred nose emblazoned on his memory.

He won his horse handily, and indeed the creature was magnificent. Daniel took the stallion away as well, only to come upon St. James a goodly way down the road, standing between his chestnut stallion and the new gelding, covered in dust and grime.

"Calhoun! Good day to you. I fear the new addition to my stable is going to tax me greatly. He has just pulled me off my horse."

He would have laughed, but St. James'

expression was at once so rueful and so amused that he could not.

"Good day to you, as well. And I suppose all I can say is that I am sure you will be a match made in heaven."

"Oh, yes, no doubt. I hate to prevail upon you, but do you think you might hold this one's lead while I attempt to mount? I fear I have damaged myself."

It lay on the tip of his tongue to refuse, but he noticed St. James did indeed favor his left leg, as if it were too sore to put weight on. Daniel sighed, tying the lead of his new stallion across his own gelding's saddle and leading his horses to tie them at a tree and keep them from tangling with Michael's.

He took the beaten gelding's reins. "Terrible what some men will do to a good horse," he remarked.

"It is. I could not abide seeing him more abused. Ah, well, perhaps Elias will like him."

Daniel gave Michael a keen look. "You would buy your manservant a horse?"

"Why on earth not? He can not drive a cart all of the time." St. James hopped about a bit until he got his balance, then worked to pull himself up.

"I see." He did not, really, but there it was; the paradox that was Michael St. James.

Michael managed to gain the saddle, a deep grimace on his face. The man did not once complain, however, which surprised Daniel as well.

He would have expected Michael to piss and moan about the injury.

He surprised himself with what he said next. "My home is closer. I would be willing to stable the gelding there and have a look at your leg."

Michael's eyebrows rose nearly to his hairline. "Are you certain? I would much appreciate it."

"I said so, didn't I?" Daniel snapped it out, and Michael seemed to relax, nodding.

"Very well, then. Lead on."

Daniel handed up the gelding's lead and went to regain his own saddle, wondering at himself. He did occasionally pride himself on being human, but being so close to this damnable man had to be a mistake, did it not?

Whatever had gotten into him?

Whatever it was that had gotten into Daniel Calhoun, it pleased Michael greatly. They stabled the horses, Michael insisting upon helping until Calhoun snapped at him to go and sit down before he fell. The addition of "you stubborn bastard" to the admonition made it no less pleasing, for it still showed concern for his welfare, which meant he was gaining ground. Really, he'd had no inkling that Daniel was even about when he made his show of buying the gelding; he'd been carried through by righteous indignation on the nag's part. But it had worked out well all around, despite his deeply sore leg.

Daniel had to help him up to the house, and while it was done reluctantly, Michael savored the feel of Daniel's arm about him, and of Daniel's body next to his, warming him against the crisp chill of the early fall day.

Daniel sat him down rather gingerly in the study, reaching for his boot. Michael could not help but hiss as it came off, and Daniel shot him a quick, concerned look. Truly, it was unfair for such a man as Calhoun to have such beautiful green eyes, such long eyelashes.

The knee of his right leg was quite swollen, as was his ankle, and bruises were already beginning to form. Daniel probed his limb, big hands as gentle as he could ask, as if he were one of Daniel's mares about to foal.

"Well, it appears you have not broken anything in your foolhardiness, St. James. Still, I would wager you will need to stay off of it for some days. I shall have a hot compress made for it."

"And a hot toddy as well?"

"Oh, for…" Daniel stood abruptly, dropping his leg on a tufted footstool. Michael winced. "Yes, all right. I shall send a man to your house if you please, let your Elias know you will be arriving by carriage and not until later in the day. It will take some time for my man to ready it all."

That was more than he expected and all he

could hope for. "Thank you, Calhoun," he said, meaning it sincerely.

"Hmph."

Daniel left him then, and a few minutes later a servant arrived with a compress and a toddy strong enough to render his new horse unconscious. Gads, the man must have the constitution of an ox if that was how he drank his own.

After consuming it and letting his leg be fussed over by a parade of footmen, maids, and perhaps even the cook, for he had never seen the stout lady who brought him tea and cakes, Michael was feeling most warm and rather tipsy, sitting happily and stroking the soft, warm fabric that covered the arms of the great chair he sat in.

"You look like a simpleton who has been given hot berry tarts."

"Ah, then hot berry tarts are your favorite, I take it?" He could not help himself. The conclusion simply popped out, making Daniel's brows lower.

"Most amusing, St. James."

"I rather thought so. I say, Calhoun, your staff is terribly accommodating. One assumes it is because you have guests so rarely."

"One assumes correctly. I have no desire to have people lying about my home, taking advantage of my good will."

He almost giggled. Really! He usually held his liquor better than that. Michael wondered just what had been in that toddy. "You have good will toward your fellow man? One would never know. Come, Calhoun, don't frown at me so. I am wounded. Call a truce, can't you?"

"I have work to do." Daniel turned on his heel, and Michael sighed. Loudly.

"I suppose I shall just be forced to grill your servants about you. I have no doubt they will be most forthcoming. I can be charming, you know."

That had exactly the effect he hoped it would, bringing Daniel right back to glare down upon him. What a picture the man presented, hands on his hips, legs planted wide, stalwart as an old oak tree. Michael wanted to eat the man whole.

"You would not dare."

"I would. I can imagine they would have all manner of stories to tell about you." Oh, that would be most entertaining. Michael wondered idly if Daniel's nanny was still alive.

"Oh, damnation." Daniel sat across from him, arms folded, lower lip sticking out mutinously. "I suppose I shall be forced to stay, then, so you are not interrogating my help."

"Lovely! Tell me a story." Michael waved an imperious hand. "Something from your childhood. And ring for another of those marvelous toddies. My goodness, whatever was in it is a sure cure for what ails me."

"It's whiskey I make here."

"How very talented you are!" Michael was positively giddy. "Another, please."

With a gleaming smile that he should have worried over, Daniel rang for another toddy, asking for one for himself as well. Michael watched the shift and pull of Daniel's muscles under his clothing with utter absorption, feeling as if someone had suddenly stirred the fire in the hearth so the heat poured over him.

"A story, hmm?"

"Yes, if you please. Something amusing."

"I thought I amused you simply by existing, St. James." The drinks arrived and Daniel sat again, sipping his. Michael gulped his rather greedily, but really, it was most extraordinary.

"I have a feeling you will be even more amusing quite soon. Very well, a story. Shall I tell you about the time Jane and I cornered a skunk?"

Michael clapped his hands in delight. "Oh, yes, please."

By the time Daniel finished the tale of his convincing Jane to try to keep a skunk as a pet, Michael had convulsed with laughter and held his stomach as he doubled over with it, tears streaming down his face. Daniel was a fine storyteller, and Michael made a point to tell him so.

"Thank you, St. James." Daniel toasted him. "Now you tell me a story."

"About what?" Michael tilted his head to one side. Calhoun was almost congenial. This new Daniel was most pleasant.

"Why did you come here?"

The over-casual question cast a pall over his happy intoxication, and Michael gave an elaborate shrug. "The suggestion to do so came rather strongly from my father."

"I see. But why here?"

"Because there is absolutely no one of any consequence to my family here, and therefore I can cause no more shame. Do you think your carriage might be ready now? I should like to go home."

The pleasant intoxication had worn right off. Michael certainly did not wish to think of his father's face when he returned home in the early hours of the day, his hand still stained with black powder, his boots spattered with mud from the dueling ground. Neither did he wish to think of his mother, sneaking in to see him even after his father forbade it, pressing a small box containing her pearls and a small fortune in silver and gold coins into his hands and kissing his cheek.

She had smelled of roses and hair powder, and she had seemed so frail suddenly. So very small.

"I am sure it is available. Come." Daniel said nothing more about his story, simply stood, holding out a hand to him.

Try as he might to disdain it, Michael was forced to take it as he stood, and the world spun about him. "Gracious, Calhoun! That whiskey is lethal."

"It's meant for men made of sterner stuff than you, St. James."

Damn it all to the fiery pits of Hell. The man

insisted on seeing him as some weak ne'er-do-well.

"Then I can see why you did not drink much of it, Calhoun." With that he attempted to sail out under his own wind, and ended up tripping over his own feet, heading for a nasty fall until Daniel caught him, holding him upright.

"Do not be stubborn, St. James. Let me help you out."

Daniel looked, and sounded, almost contrite. Must be due to the whiskey, and Michael had just enough rake in him to take advantage of it. He leaned heavily against Daniel's warm, firm frame, rubbing gently along one side of the man. Oh, much better than being angry.

"Very well, Calhoun. But only because you deliberately got me in this state."

"Yes, yes, as you say."

The carriage indeed awaited him, the coachman sitting patiently atop. Michael tried to plant his foot upon the step and missed, laughing a little as he staggered. He tried again, and Daniel made an impatient noise.

"I swear, St. James, you are beyond anything."

"Well, if you would help me. Perhaps if you got in the carriage and pulled me up."

"Oh, for Heaven's sake."

Daniel did just that, though, getting up in the carriage and holding a hand out. Taking that large, square hand, Michael let himself be pulled into the interior, falling against Daniel, hands landing upon Daniel'swide chest.

The moment was almost too much, almost too much like an Italian farce, and yet how cold he not take full advantage? He leaned up and kissed Daniel full on the mouth, finding Daniel did indeed taste exactly the way he remembered, cinnamon and cloves, and in this instance, whiskey.

Daniel made a sound, too, just as he had the last time, a cross between outrage and surprise. Michael fully expected to have to take his lumps, assuming Daniel would once more flatten him, but to his shock, Daniel grabbed him by the upper arms and pulled him closer, kissing him so harshly he felt his lips swelling, felt bruises pop up along his skin where Daniel held him.

They broke apart, and Michael stared, Daniel having done something for once that truly shocked him. He rubbed his fingers over his lips.

"You kissed me back."

Daniel stared at him, green eyes glinting oddly. "I did," he rejoined.

"Why?"

Daniel laughed, the sound harsh, as he climbed down out of the carriage, leaving Michael sprawled inelegantly. "Because you were right. I liked it."

As soon as the carriage rolled away, St. James' horses led behind by one of his grooms, Daniel called for his new stallion to be saddled. He had planned to stay and do some work, but after his encounter with that damnable St. James, he determined a need to go into town to visit Molly at the pub.

St. James confounded him, but no more than his own behavior confounded him. What was he thinking?

Of course, the way his cock strained as he mounted his horse, perhaps it was more that he was not thinking at all. Not one bit.

Neither Sally nor Molly were available when he arrived at the pub, and it was with ill grace indeed that Daniel accepted the invitation of some of the local planters to sit with them while they had luncheon.

"So, what did you think of that St. James fellow buying a worthless nag at auction, Daniel?" Master Freelow asked.

Would it not just be his luck that they would want to talk about his nemesis. How dramatic of him to think of St. James that way, when really the man was a petty annoyance. No more than a fly. That was how Daniel would think of him from now on. Surely he would think no more on that kiss. Either one.

"I commend him for doing something selfless for a change."

"You hold a low opinion of him, don't you, Daniel?"

"I hold anyone who lives a life of leisure and

never does a day of honest work in contempt, as well you know it, Samuel."

Samuel Laidlaw was one of the few of Daniel's peers he could tolerate, and he gave Daniel a grin. "Amazing how you manage to spend so much time with him then, hmm?"

Daniel gave Samuel a dampening look. "Jane insists he and I shall be friends."

Samuel just laughed, puffing on his pipe. "Yes, Jane must be pacified at all costs. I must say, she looked radiant when I saw her last at your soiree, Daniel. I was glad to see it."

"As was I." Daniel smiled his thanks. Jane had few enough friends. It was good to see Samuel support her.

"Never could understand why Gerard married the chit myself." Henry Barstow stood next to their table, adjusting the cuff of his ridiculously fine coat. His tone was utterly offensive, and, sadly, he had not St. James' charm to soften the blow. Daniel looked him over slowly, from the newly fashionable cutaway coat that showed his truss to the wispy hair meant to look like the ancient busts of Caesar and instead looked like the man had been caught in a gale.

"Yes, well, I have seen your wife, sirrah, and can see Jane would not be to your taste."

Smoke poured out of Samuel's nostrils as he choked. Freelow gurgled into his ale, and Barstow merely drew himself up tightly as he answered, "Yes, indeed. One can hardly compare a thoroughbred to a plow horse."

"Nor a plow horse to a sway-backed mare past her prime, indeed."

He simply would not have it. Daniel was not one to back down from a fight, especially with an upstart like Barstow. And he might not be the most popular man in the parish, but against someone such as this man, his neighbors would stand with him. As was evidenced by Samuel.

"Perhaps you ought to have a solitary drink today, Henry. Jane is quite a favorite of mine," Samuel said.

Barstow grunted, a harrumphing sound, and left with ill grace. Samuel pointed after him with the stem of his pipe.

"Now there is a ne'er-do-well, Daniel."

"Oh, I don't know," Freelow said. "He simply seems to dislike Daniel and family. One can understand it, if one is from elsewhere." Freelow looked at him apologetically. "Your family is unconventional, Daniel, and Jane is an original."

"Yes, well, I should think he would have more opportunity to meet such people in the city, hmm?"

Daniel drank his ale down and finished his plate. This outing had been less than useless. He should have done better with his own hand as company. His cheeks reddened at the thought of touching himself, which he had been taught was self-abuse. Still, the idea appealed, even if he thought St. James would intrude upon his thoughts that way.

Eventually he simply left, saying a brusque goodbye to his neighbors and ignoring Molly as she came down the narrow back stairs adjusting her apron. Somehow she seemed less than appealing. He wondered why he had ever seen fit to frequent her bed.

Then he wondered whatever had come over him when Michael St. James was more attractive to him than a woman's soft curves.

He must be going mad. Surely he could lay that blame on Michael St. James, as well.

Chapter Five

The harvest came fine that year, the crops bountiful, for which Daniel was grateful. Farming was a debtor's game, and he needed the crop sales to be able to pay off his liens. Gerard and Jane did well, also, though Gerard was wealthy enough to make a play at it only.

Still, a finished, and successful, harvest meant a festival. The day of the festival dawned bright and almost warm, only the slight edge of frost on the yellowing grasses indicating how cold it had been the last fortnight, causing them all to rush to get the crops in.

Daniel attended because Jane insisted and because those people who worked his crops deserved the day, deserved to see he approved their efforts. Daniel employed freedmen at Jane's insistence, a practice that made him ever less popular among his peers, but he found it to be more productive and less expensive than indentured servants or slaves.

Still, that meant a certain amount of care must be taken to make sure they came back in the spring to work.

Daniel strolled through the crowds, his coat flapping about his legs as he nodded at all and sundry. Many of his people were there, and Daniel stopped to give them each a few coins, a few words of praise. It took no time really, and Jane was right, it was well worth the happy smiles he received.

If he found himself searching the faces in the crowd around him for a certain pair of whiskey eyes and not finding them, then so be it.

He'd taken an ale with Samuel, had shared a pie with Jane, and was just about to take his leave when he heard the hail.

"Hoy, Calhoun!"

He turned, and surely enough it was Michael St. James, looking well recovered from his fall, mahogany hair shining and unhatted in the fall sunshine. His whole body tightened, and Daniel called himself all manner of fool. The things he contemplated with Michael were illegal as well as immoral.

He began as he would continue. Fighting. "St. James, really, I did not think you would find our quaint country fair to your taste."

"You would be surprised by what entertains me, my dear."

His what? Daniel stared, and Michael gifted him with a beatific smile. It was maddening.

"You go too far, St. James. My name is Calhoun, as we have discussed before."

"Of course." The smile did not change, save

for a look in St. James' eyes, something dark and dangerous flashing there. "I beg your pardon. Will you walk with me?"

"Whatever for?"

"Well, if you prefer I discuss our last meeting here…"

"I do not see why you insist upon discussing it. However, if you must, we will do so far from here."

Daniel turned on his heel and strode away, leaving St. James to follow. Damnable man. Such things he said and did. Daniel felt like punching him again, except they were in public, and for Jane's sake he would not cause a scene. Oh, yes, and for his own. He still must live in the parish after St. James' exile was over.

They wandered down the dirt road out of the crowds of people, beyond where the fire pits were producing the famed Harvest ox roast. When they were finally out of sight beyond the hill, Daniel turned, hands upon his hips.

"Well?" he asked.

"Well," Michael said, stepping forward. "I really did not wish to speak to you."

St. James was right before him, so close that Daniel could feel the heat of him, even through layers of velvet and broadcloth. Closer and closer Michael moved until suddenly their lips met, Michael's hand cupping his cheek, fingers trailing next to his ear.

A thousand wild thoughts careened through

his mind—the very public nature of the kiss, the audacity of St. James for even attempting such a thing, the unbelievable softness of Michael's lips. Daniel found himself returning the kiss, very much against his better judgment, and enjoying it to boot.

When Michael pressed close and he felt the shocking evidence of a man's arousal against his thigh, however, Daniel broke away.

"I do not even like you, St. James."

St. James nodded in return, hands falling to his sides. Those clear amber eyes had gone dark, slumberous. "I am well aware, Calhoun. However, it is entirely unnecessary for you to like me."

Daniel shook his head, disbelief warring with temptation. "I am no sodomite."

Instead of producing indignation, that got him a wicked smile. "How do you know unless you try it?"

"Damn you. How do you do this to me?"

"This" was the surge in his blood, the very imperative that he had to try it, and only with Michael St. James. That smile infuriated him, made violence boil in his veins, and Daniel reached for Michael again, hands closing hard on Michael's arms.

"I hate you."

"I know," Michael said and kissed him like there was no consequence to be paid, as if there would be no regret tomorrow.

How could he not try to take control of that

kiss? Daniel was a man used to being the aggressor, used to taking what he wanted, and he pulled Michael against him, pushing his tongue in to taste Michael's mouth.

Astounding, the way St. James melted into him, the way those arms flew up about his neck. The sound of his name as a moan on Michael's lips excited him unbearably, and before Daniel even knew it, they had sunk to the ground, cold and muddy beneath his knees, and were kissing deeply, both of them clutching the other's back.

His prick was hard, hard and hot, pushing against his breeches, against Michael's hip. Daniel simply could not fathom it, and so he stopped trying, only feeling for a time. When Michael slipped a hand between them to touch him through the cloth that separated them, Daniel thought he might well have found Heaven.

He felt like an untried youth, truly, for he pushed into that touch, all control lost at the very feel of it. Michael seemed just as affected by it, moaning into his kiss, fingers tracing his entire length and breadth before finding the buttons under the flap of his trous and working to free him. Daniel was scandalized.

"St. James! You go too far… Someone could see."

"Nonsense. Who will come this far out but fools like us? Let me touch you, Daniel." The heat in Michael's voice, the entreaty, made him nod.

Hot, firm, Michael's hand found his shaft, closing about it, and Daniel lost the ability to speak, lost the need to do anything but arch into the touch, panting for his very breath. They kissed again, and his lip split under the pressure, the taste of blood oddly strong.

Daniel could no longer hold it in, and with a cry he climaxed, his seed spilling out over Michael's hand, falling to the cold ground to mix with the mud.

Michael only smiled at him, raising his hand to his mouth in what must be the most erotic gesture Daniel had ever witnessed, licking it clean. All he could do was stare. "Did you… I mean, have you?"

"Yes," Michael replied, rather ruefully. "I fear I have. I shall have to make my escape the long way, so no one might see my state. Come with me?"

"No."

The bald refusal did not seem to surprise St. James much. The infuriating fellow simply nodded.

"I thought you might refuse. Do not think it will keep me from pursuing you, my dear. I have every intention of this, or something very like it, happening again. Soon." Michael's hands shook, the only indication that he was as affected as Daniel.

"And I intend to thwart you at every turn." Daniel stood on shaky legs, brushing as much of the thick, loamy mud off as he could.

"Of course you do. It would not be a challenge if you did not, and I love nothing more than a challenge."

St. James rose as well, looking rumpled and frayed at the edges, but still unutterably elegant. Then the man had the audacity to come to him and kiss the corner of his mouth.

"Should you find, Calhoun, that you crave my company before I mount my next salvo, you know where I reside. Until then, farewell."

With that St. James took himself off, leaving Daniel feeling bereft, angry and quite frankly, bewildered.

Truly, he would never underestimate Michael St. James again.

Michael decided, not long after the encounter in the muddy field, that his next salvo would indeed be to let Daniel Calhoun come to him.

Waiting was one of the most difficult things he had ever done, for now he had the feel of Daniel's skin firmly in his mind, the taste of Daniel's seed on his tongue. How he longed for more.

He paced his front room, his boot heels catching on the threadbare carpet that was once delicate and lovely, undoubtedly, but to him looked shabby. Michael sighed. Surely someday he would become accustomed to his reduced circumstances.

He should go riding. He was dressed for it, and it was a lovely fall day, the leaves outside a bright hue, the sun shining, only the barest hint of cold in the air. The thing he feared, however, was that once he got going, he would point his mount toward Daniel Calhoun and not stop riding until he found the man.

So, instead, he paced. He called for a bath, then changed his mind. He sat and wrote a letter to his mother, telling her how his situation was improved by finding a like-minded companion. That gave him satisfaction for long moments, thinking how his father would panic at the very idea.

Finally, Michael gave up, calling for Elias to have his stallion saddled. He would go to Daniel and rejoin the hunt, for he found himself craving Daniel's voice and the look in those mossy green eyes as Daniel shuddered out his completion.

He got to the door and opened it, intending a great, dramatic exit and was forced to stop short instead, as Daniel Calhoun stood on his doorstep, scowling thunderously at him.

Well, well. No, this was an unexpected pleasure. Michael hid a smile. "Calhoun! How lovely to see you. What may I do for you?"

Daniel looked about, gesturing for him to precede Daniel inside. He did, calling for Elias to have one of the grooms exercise his horse.

"Have I interrupted your outing, St. James?" Daniel asked, his tone brusque.

"Not at all. Please. Come and sit."

They went to the drawing room, and Michael sat on the settee, watching Daniel move about the room, touching this ornament or that. He did not think he had ever seen Daniel Calhoun so unsettled. He could hardly wait to see what Daniel had to say.

"Oh. Well…"

Daniel would not look at him, at least not directly. Instead, he kept sneaking glances out of the corners of his eyes. Feeling somewhat cruel and very aroused, Michael leaned back, stretching his booted feet out in front of him, legs spread to show his assets to their best advantage. "I assume you have come to berate me for something, Calhoun. Please do get on with it. The suspense is more than I can bear."

"Oh, do shut it, St. James. You know perfectly well why I am here."

Oh, that flush, whether from rage or embarrassment, was entirely too delicious. Michael savored the way it lit Daniel's cheeks, the way it brought out sparks of pure emerald in Daniel's eyes.

"Do I? I think perhaps I am not as well informed as you think me, my dear."

"Stop that."

"What?"

"Calling me 'my dear.' And I want to know why."

"Why what?"

Daniel made a noise of pure impatience, sounding very much like a growl. Michael thrilled to it, his prick immediately firming. What a joy this man was to all of his senses.

"Why do you insist upon pursuing me? I have told you I am no sodomite, St. James. And yet you…I… Damnation."

He raised his brows in mock surprise. "Now, Daniel. It has been some days since I even raised a finger in your direction. I think perhaps you have it backward. You are the one here, at my home, yes?"

"Damn you." Daniel strode to him, boot heels thumping on the floor. "Damn you to Hell and back, St. James."

Such fire. How thrilling. Utterly captivating. "No doubt I am damned for all eternity. I daresay it's more entertaining than being good all of the time."

Those eyes snapped green fire, Daniel's chest rising and falling in agitation. "How do you do it, St. James? How do you make me want…these things you do?"

Michael stood abruptly, forcing Daniel to back up a pace. He reached out, touching that bristly cheek, noting that no razor had touched Daniel Calhoun's face this day. The contrast between his skin and Daniel's was rather shocking, pale against dark.

"If I do force this upon you, Daniel, I can only say I do it out of the strength of my longing for you. If you find that…inspiring, then so be it."

"I don't want this," Daniel said, shaking his head roughly.

"I know. But you need it."

"The Devil take you."

Michael smiled. "I would rather you did."

Daniel groaned. "Be careful what you wish for, St. James."

With that he was suddenly in Daniel's arms, surrounded by the sheer, brute strength of the man as Daniel bent and kissed him, rough and deep. Michael moaned, opening for the kiss, clutching Daniel as the world spun about him. Oh, yes. Just yes.

When the kiss ended they were on their knees, clinging to one another, both of them whooping for air. He could not help but stare at Daniel, searching that blunt face. What he saw there was raw need, tempered by a fine anger. It aroused him like nothing else.

He took another kiss, aggressive, pushing deep into Daniel's mouth with his tongue. Daniel opened for him, letting him taste and explore. Those huge hands closed upon his hips, pulling him close, and Michael moaned again at the feel of Daniel's hardness against him. He could not begin to explain how the knowledge that Daniel wanted him despite himself affected him.

They kissed feverishly, and Michael only realized he was waiting for Daniel to do something, anything, when his hands found Daniel's buttons and began to tug at them. Of course Daniel would not know exactly what to do with him. He was a man, after all. Perhaps it was time Michael showed him some of the things men might do together.

He struggled with Daniel's coat, as it was trapped beneath their legs, but got it, the frock coat and waistcoat off before starting in the fine lawn shirt. Catching his hands, Daniel drew back, looking at him.

"Your servants…"

"Know when I need my privacy. I have not the patience for the trip above stairs, short though it may be."

Michael slapped Daniel's hands away, tugging at the shirt and trousers, finally baring Daniel to his hungry gaze. What a work of art the man was. Broad shoulders tapered into a narrow waist, the skin of chest and thighs sprinkled liberally with dark hair. Daniel's shaft was most magnificent, though. It stood away from Daniel's body, flushed a deep red, the foreskin pulled back, silvery drops leaking from the slit.

How could he not touch it? Michael wrapped his fingers around Daniel's prick, feeling it quiver under his touch, seeing the muscles in Daniel's belly pull tight. Such muscles. Only a man who labored hard could have the like, and Michael scooted back, bending to lick at them, rubbing his cheek against the ridges.

"St. James!"

"Mmm?" Not to be distracted, Michael bent even more and took the head of Daniel's prick into his mouth, licking, lips closing tight about it. Daniel shouted, thighs like stone beneath his hands, and began to thrust up into his mouth and throat.

"Michael. What are you... it's unnatural. Michael."

The last came out as encouragement, he felt, a heartfelt plea, and Michael answered it with enthusiasm, sucking his way to the root of Daniel's prick, fingers sliding up the tender insides of Daniel's thighs to cup his heavy balls in one hand. Had anything ever tasted as fine as Daniel Calhoun? Smelled as rich?

Daniel made noises as Michael labored, deep and needy, sounds that seemed torn from deep in his chest and belly. They were as opium to Michael and he took them in greedily, just as he did the bitter drops that slid along his tongue. Soon, he thought. Soon. With that he slid one finger back along behind Daniel's sac, pressing the sensitive skin there hard, and even as he sucked one last time, Daniel cried out and filled him, shooting hard down his greedy throat.

Michael sat up quickly, leaning in while Daniel was still dazed and blinking from his little death, taking a kiss that had Daniel spluttering then moaning and kissing him back, taking in his own taste. Practically crawling atop Daniel, Michael rubbed his hard prick against Daniel's leg, needing touch, needing so badly.

One of Daniel's hand came to rest on his

bottom, pulling him close, and Michael moaned again, reaching for Daniel's other hand and pressing it between them.

"Please. Daniel."

He was not above begging if necessary. Not at all. To his everlasting surprise, Daniel did as he asked, nay, went one step further and opened his placket, blunt fingers slipping inside his breeches to find his swollen length and pet it gently. Too gently.

Pushing desperately into the touch, Michael bit down on the skin of Daniel's neck, just below the ear. "Harder, Daniel. Touch me as you would yourself."

The touch deepened, Daniel stroking him roughly now, the calluses on Daniel's fingers scraping his most sensitive skin. Michael cried out, his eyes fairly rolling back in his head as he spent, his entire body convulsing with it. Yes. Oh, goodness, yes.

They simply sat there for the longest time, breathing heavily, Daniel still clutching him in one hand. The gesture seemed possessive, and Michael took that as a good sign. A very good sign indeed. He leaned his head on Daniel's shoulder, fingers tracing idle patterns on Daniel's skin.

"Will you come abovestairs now, Calhoun, and spend the day with me?"

Daniel snorted, the sound amused and inelegant. "I haven't the time to fritter away an entire day dallying with you, St. James."

"Of course not. But will you anyway?"

To his everlasting surprise, Daniel nodded, lips moving against his hair. "Yes, St. James. I will."

"Damnation, Jane, stop laughing at me. You are a lady. Should you not be appalled at such things?"

Daniel paced while Jane sat with her babe at her breast, looking like a Madonna painted by some old master. A goodly two-thirds of the county was horrified by her steadfast refusal to have a wet nurse, though what business it was of theirs, Daniel did not know. Gerard thought it endearing, which only reinforced Daniel's liking of the man.

While he paced and waited for an answer, Jane moved the child from one breast to another, the soft smacking sounds the babe made forcing a smile from him.

"Oh, come now, Daniel. You know I have never been conventional." She smiled for him, and he looked for strain but found none.

"Jane, this goes beyond defying convention, and you know it."

She simply looked at him, eyes clear and serious. "I know it. And perhaps I should be appalled at that. Heaven knows, everyone one else in three counties would be. But well, damnation, Daniel. I like him."

"Jane!" Daniel opened his eyes very wide,

attempting a scandalized mien, making her laugh so hard the baby burped.

"You play the innocent very poorly, Daniel."

"Yes, yes, I know. Now, tell me. What am I to do?"

He really did wish she could do so. Daniel had not the first inkling of what to do about Michael St. James. The man was addiction, plain and simple, and in the last weeks, Daniel had spent more time in St. James' bed than in his own. Naturally, he refused to let it affect his work, his land, but otherwise, St. James had quite taken over his life, and to his own surprise, Daniel had let him, and happily at that.

It had to be unnatural. Sinful. Wrong. Did it not?

"Oh, Daniel. I wish I could. I truly do. But I cannot, and you know it. You care for him, yes?"

"He is a ne'er-do-well and a scoundrel." And a cast-out who would someday leave to go back to his fine city life. Daniel knew that well enough. When Michael St. James left it might break him. "Besides, even if I did, which I am not saying I do, nothing could come of it, Jane."

She nodded, shifting on her perch, her pale skin shining where her dress gaped. "I know, Daniel. It will cause little but pain for you if you continue in this. And yet, what is life without taking chances?"

Daniel turned on his heel to start pacing again, the thick rug Gerard had brought in from somewhere up north muffling his footsteps. Really, the man spoiled Jane to death. Daniel smiled at the idea. Thank God.

"I have taken some very great chances of late. I am not sure I am willing to take more."

"It is not like you to vacillate so, Daniel. Either you will continue or you will not." The nanny came in just as the child finished eating and took his newest cousin away to sleep while Jane straightened her dress, coming to him and laying a hand on his arm. "Perhaps you should try to ascertain how he feels?"

Shrugging his shoulders, Daniel turned away. St. James undoubtedly felt he was nothing but a challenge. A divertissement. Jane turned him back with a soft touch, her hazel eyes showing nothing but love and concern.

"You might at least ask."

"That is not my way, and you know it."

"Then break it off," she told him. "Do not toy with him."

The stubborn set of her chin, so like his, made Daniel smile. "I do not know if I have the strength."

"Oh." She stamped her foot at him. "Then take your lumps and shut up about it, Daniel Calhoun. If you want him, you must work for him. And have care no one but me knows of it. Yes?"

Daniel sighed, patting her hand. That was the simple truth, wasn't it? He would work for Michael St. James. Perhaps it was his turn to take up the challenge. Even if he was uncertain as to what he would do with the man when he was well and truly caught.

"Yes. Shall we play chess, now you've done your matronly duty?"

The men of his acquaintance would laugh at the idea of Jane playing chess. The truth was she was a ruthless strategist, and he needed the practice were he to beat Michael on a regular basis.

Jane laughed, the sound light and gay. "We shall. I shall pound you to a pulp."

Daniel laughed as well, feeling better now that he'd made a decision. "That is a challenge I will happily take up."

The challenge of Michael St. James would no doubt be less than happy in its outcome. But Daniel was determined to see it through, no matter what.

"Really, Calhoun, this weather is dreadful. Why did you wish to go riding again?"

The mud sucked at the hooves of Michael's horse, making it slow going, even on the high road, and as he adjusted his hat a rivulet of freezing water ran down Michael's neck. He shivered, shaking like a cat, trying to remove more water as delicately as possible.

Daniel Calhoun, on the other hand, looked like a giant retriever, happy and smiling in the face of the mist and muck. It made Michael's teeth clench.

"I thought you would be pleased to spend time with me, St. James. Especially as I suggested it."

"If I did not think it was motivated by a mean-spirited urge to see my discomfort, Calhoun, I might be pleased."

Damn it, there was more water, spilling down the side of his throat. He shook it off, and he would vow Daniel's smile widened. Bastard.

"Perhaps, St. James, I am simply getting you wet so I can take you home and dry you out before a fire, and with perhaps a glass of brandy."

Oh, now that sounded most congenial. Michael opened his mouth to agree when the clop of hooves stopped him, and he and Daniel both turned their mounts to the far side of the road to get out of the way of whatever came upon them.

Damnation. It was Henry Barstow, looking as corpulent as ever, and his skinny bird of a wife, Madeline. Who would ever have thought she could ride? They drew abreast, and Barstow looked between Michael and Daniel, bushy brows drawn. Madeline simply looked sly, eyes as bright and beady as a bird's.

"Ho, there, St. James. Surely did not expect to see you out and about this day."

Michael inclined his head, assuming the obnoxious air he had left off of late, thanks to Calhoun. "Indeed. One would scarce expect to see you and your missus out on such a day, either."

"We're on our way to Pastor Lawrence's for dinner."

"Really?" Michael slanted a look at Madeline. "Did you get saved then, dear lady?"

Madeline drew herself up, almost managing to look prim. "I have always been of a religious bent, Michael."

'Twas all he could do not to snort his derision. "As you say."

Curious eyes flitting from him to Daniel, Madeline licked her lips as if preparing for a feast. "How odd to see the two of you together so amiable."

"Not at all." Daniel said it easily, smoothly, and Michael stared. Goodness, the man could be urbane when he chose. He waited for the fatal blow. It came in less than a heartbeat. "I daresay St. James and I have more in common than you do with the good Pastor."

"I say, Calhoun. That is my wife you insult."

"Which proves I have a fine sense of social irony. Now if you will excuse us, St. James is going to look at one of my mounts for the derby next year. He's a fine mudder, and today would be the day to test him."

They rode away, Daniel's back ramrod straight, and Michael could not help but admire it. He was still staring at Daniel when they pulled up out of earshot. Daniel looked at him askance.

"What?"

"What a clever liar you are, Calhoun."

One black walnut eyebrow rose, a truly evil light

shining in those green eyes. "Who says I am lying? You have proven to be a fine mudder." Those well-cut cheeks flushed a deep rose. "And I have no doubt you will make a fine mount."

A thrill went through Michael. Surely Daniel was suggesting… they had not tried it. Not yet. The one time he had suggested it, Daniel had utterly panicked, balking at the very thought.

"Would you like to try me now?"

"Yes. I think I would, St. James."

With that, Daniel spurred away from him, racing not toward Michael's home, but toward Daniel's farm, where they had rarely spent time together. Heart pounding like his stallion's hooves, Michael followed, determined not to let Daniel get so far ahead that he would have time to think.

This was a race he intended to win.

Daniel unsaddled his horse and walked him out, eschewing the groom's help. Good Gad, what had gotten into him?

Prurient curiosity, that had to be it. Such emotion would no doubt be his downfall one day. Ever since St. James had mentioned, well, that Daniel had wanted to, and yet he could not help but think it unnatural. Tantalizing, but unnatural.

Still, he did not think St. James would let it die now. Perhaps that was a good thing, for if they tried it, and he found it distasteful, they would never be forced to do it again.

Michael clattered up just as Daniel finished stabling his mount.

"Did you get lost, St. James?" he asked, looking up to see Michael, filthy and spattered with mud. "You had a fall!"

He moved to help Michael dismount, chagrined at the very concern he felt.

"Not a bad one. My mount slipped and sent me scrambling. I swear you will think I am a terrible horseman."

"Not at all." He had seen St. James ride more than once, and if the man could win a derby... "Undoubtedly you are simply used to better conditions."

Michael looked at him, whiskey eyes bright, indeed, dancing. "I believe that was a compliment, Daniel Calhoun. Perhaps the first you have ever paid me out of bed."

He felt his cheeks heat. "Nonsense. It was not an insult, is all. Come, let me call for a bath for you."

"A bath? Goodness. I cannot decide, Calhoun, if your solicitousness is due to kindness, or to a desire to delay the inevitable."

"The inevitable? I have no idea what you mean."

Damn the man for pushing and pushing. Daniel all but carried Michael to the house, calling for a hot bath. Michael merely watched all of preparations with a predatory sort of smile. Unnerving, it was, and Daniel finally called him down on it.

"I wish you would stop staring," Daniel muttered.

"I beg your pardon. You are simply most endearing when nervous, my dear."

Really, he was never sure if he should snarl or blush when Michael called him that. "I am not nervous!"

Snarling won out, and Daniel jerked Michael up off the settle he had sat on, hauling him up the stairs to his dressing room so he might strip off the mud-spattered clothes while they waited for water to heat.

Daniel undressed St. James like a child, and Michael let him, hands hanging loose at his sides. The body he uncovered was not that of a child, though, pale and lean muscled and darkened in places with hair much deeper in color than that on Michael's head. The hard shaft he encountered was not that of a boy's either, and while it still made him blush, it also made him proud he had made the hardness so.

He looked into Michael's eyes as he wrapped one hand about that straining prick. "Shall I keep you from getting cold while you wait for your bath?"

Those odd amber eyes went wide, Michael's lips opening on a gasp. Daniel's own prick jumped as Michael licked his lips, tongue pink and wet.

"Oh, yes, please. That would be lovely."

Feeling very bold indeed, Daniel stroked the shaft, really letting himself enjoy it. Oh, he had held it before, stroked it roughly, but he had not really taken the time to feel how smooth the skin was, how hot. His fingers traced the large veins, played with the looser texture of the foreskin, drew that back to dip into the slit.

All the while Michael watched him, his gaze burning with bright fire. Small noises began to issue forth, deep and needy, rough sounds that drove him on. Daniel looked down, and the sight of his hand wrapped so intimately around Michael was more arousing than he could have imagined. He moaned, leaning to kiss Michael deeply and be kissed in return.

Daniel drew his thumb down the underside of Michael's prick, eliciting another gasp, and bent to bite deep into the join of Michael's neck and shoulder, something Michael had done to him many times. Somehow, being clothed while Michael was nude gave him a feeling of equilibrium, took his usual nervousness away. Yes, he had it, despite denying it.

Clutching at him, Michael encouraged Daniel with words and movements. Filthy words, in fact, some he had never heard during even the most intense sessions with Molly or Sally, words that made him moan. Michael moved into his touch, pushing that swollen prick into his fist, and he squeezed, groaning happily as Michael spent over his fingers, practically wailing his name.

To know he had just as much power over St. James as the man had over him was a heady thing indeed.

"Well," he said, looking at Michael's flushed face. "You certainly seem to have warmed nicely."

"Your method is uniquely effective, yes."

Dazed as Michael appeared to be, he could still snap right back. Most admirable, though Daniel would never tell him that. A soft knock on the door announced the bath was ready, and Daniel left Michael for a moment to usher the maid out of his bedchamber and latch the door from the inside.

"Your bath awaits," he called, and Michael sauntered out, naked as the day he was born, testing the water with his hand and smiling.

"Oh, excellent. You will join me, I trust?"

"Certainly. Shall I wash your back?"

"What an accommodating mood you are in!" He got a kiss for his efforts, Michael teasing him with lips and tongue before stepping into the water and sinking down with a happy sigh. "Really, you have a purely decadent tub, Calhoun. I must get one."

Daniel felt his cheeks heat, and he was glad for being behind St. James so he could not see it. "I am rather a large man, St. James. It would not be comfortable to have a small tub."

"True. Come, Calhoun. Undress and join me. I will not hurt you."

Oh, the tone was maddening, used as though he were some blushing maid how had never been with another. Daniel stripped off his neckcloth, grumbling. "I vow, St. James, you are most disagreeable."

"Well, one of us must be, and as you are not right now…"

He smacked St. James with his coat as he took it off, gaining a shout of laughter for his troubles. Finally he was nude and he moved about to step into the tub opposite St. James, glaring the man down.

"Well, how are you to wash my back from over there?"

"You have cheated yourself out of that, St. James, with your snide tongue."

"You thought my tongue clever enough the other day…"

Daniel raised a brow, splashing water at Michael's chest. "You have no shame."

"No, indeed. Now let us bathe so we can continue on with the more entertaining part of the day." Those eyes went hot, Michael's toes sliding up his leg under the water. "I would have you inside me, Daniel."

His cock leapt, and Daniel swallowed hard, picking up the pine-scented soap he favored and moving close so he might scrub them both thoroughly. Despite Michael's admonitions for haste, Daniel took his time, learning Michael's body under the guise of searching out and eradicating all traces of mud. Apparently, Michael was horribly ticklish, not on his ribs, but where his thighs joined his body. His belly was flat and the curves of his hipbones sharp, and his nipples were so sensitive even the rasp of the old cloth Daniel used on them made Michael gasp and twist.

They rinsed off, and Daniel stood, water running off him in sheets. He held out his hand, loving the hungry look St. James spared him, feeling it like a physical touch.

"Come on, St. James. You shall have your inevitable," Daniel said, his nerves jittering.

"I cannot wait."

Hand in his, St. James rose, and they went together to the big bed, climbing up into it and stretching out together. A thought occurred to Daniel before they got too comfortable, however.

"Will we need something to ease the way?"

"Good man." Michael smiled and kissed the corner of his mouth. "Have you any oil?"

"I do." He rolled away to get it, feeling Michael's eyes on him again, feeling ridiculous with his prick bobbing about as he walked. Still, St. James seemed to find it arousing rather than amusing, if the way he was attacked when he reached the bed again was any indication.

Michael pushed him down and straddled him, taking the lead, which was as odd as it was exciting for Daniel, who was used to blushes and sighs with the occasional farm girl and practiced boredom from barmaids like Molly. Bending, Michael brought their mouths together, pushing into his mouth, tongue performing a parody of the act to come.

His prick dragged along Michael's thigh and belly, Michael's shaft coming to rest against his as they moved. 'Twas like nothing else ever. Michael touched him all over, the need almost invasive, but so good that Daniel could not complain. Not a bit. Daniel touched St. James in turn, hands cupping the masculine curves of Michael's buttocks and squeezing.

"Get the oil, Daniel," Michael demanded.

He blinked, but complied, grabbing the oil from where he'd sat it, staring at Michael. Michael smiled, the look as gentle as any he'd ever had bestowed on him.

"Now, coat your fingers with it. You will need to prepare me."

His hands shook a bit as he unstoppered the oil and coated his fingers with it, and Daniel cursed himself as a fool. It should be much easier with a man, damn it all. Why was he so worried? He got three fingers good and wet and set the oil aside, reaching behind Michael to set one at the entrance to Michael's body.

"Yes. Just that way, Calhoun. Now, gently push inside. I am ready."

Michael did look ready indeed, eyes practically glowing, hair falling about his face, cheeks flushed. Daniel pushed, found resistance, and nearly gave up. Instead, Michael pressed back on his finger, and suddenly it slipped right inside. Daniel's eyes widened; Michael was as hot inside as the hinges of Hell. God above.

They moved, him pushing inside Michael with one and then two fingers, Michael bracing against his chest and pulling him deeper with each rock of his hips. Daniel was about to introduce a third finger when Michael rose up, allowing Daniel's fingers to slip free, and reached for the oil.

"I cannot wait, Daniel."

Moving quickly, Michael poured oil into his hand while Daniel watched then reached down and stroked it over Daniel's prick, making him gasp and arch. Before Daniel could even blink, Michael was moving up, reaching back to settle the head of Daniel's prick against that stretched hole, and Daniel was sliding right in without even the least bit of a struggle.

Hot. Tight. Slick. Daniel moaned, the sound surprising him with its intensity, his hips rising immediately as he tried to get more of the sensation. He thought he might die a happy man, right there beneath Michael St. James.

Wouldn't the parish be agog at that?

When Michael began moving, he lost all control, and all Daniel could do was to hold on to Michael's hips and thrust, his head falling back, breath coming in short gasps. Michael was the same, bobbing up and down, grunting, fingers digging into Daniel's skin.

He was close, feeling the impending climax rising up his spine, when he pulled Michael down to kiss his mouth, pushing deep and hard.

"St. James…"

"Michael."

Daniel blinked up, barely able to focus his eyes. "What?"

Lifting one of his hands and bringing it to the straining cock trapped between them, Michael bit his lower lip before grating out, "Do you think you might call me Michael?"

He smiled, squeezing hard on Michael's cock, pushing up as his seed began to rush from his body. "Michael!"

Sighing, Michael joined him in his pleasure, hot seed spilling over Daniel's hand as Michael tightened around him so he thought they might never come apart. They would simply be joined forever.

Then St. James collapsed upon him, breathing heavily, utterly boneless against his chest, and Daniel let go of Michael's cock in favor of stroking his back.

"Thank you, Daniel," St. James said, and all he could do was nod.

Daniel thought there was a very good chance they would be doing that again. And soon.

Chapter Six

The church was lit with seemingly hundreds of candles, the congregation all holding them as they sang. Michael found the service somewhat quaint but entirely heartfelt, and he enjoyed it more than he had enjoyed any church service in his memory.

He sat with Jane and Gerard, Daniel on the far side of them. People had talked when he arrived, and even more had whispered when he sat with the Gentry family, but Jane and Daniel's other cousins had greeted him warmly, and that was enough.

Still, Michael wished he might sit at Daniel's side.

The service went a long way toward relieving his unaccustomed melancholy. Early in the week he had received a missive from his mother, along with a goodly sum of money, explaining his father was in no way ready to forgive him, even at this most loving and forgiving time of year. She missed him, she said, and she loved him.

Of course. Too bad his father did not.

Still, he could hardly feel sorry for himself when the promise of mulled wine and a late night repast awaited him and Daniel at his home. As for his Christmas dinner, it would come in the form of supper at Jane and Gerard's on the morrow, and he had been promised goose. Complaints would be untoward and ungrateful.

They all stood for the last hymn, and Michael sang with gusto, helping Jane and Daniel drown out Gerard, who was positively dreadful.

When the last note ended, they all filed out, and he and Daniel were most careful not to drift too close together, though the temptation was great. Instead they mingled, and Michael could easily tell from the set of Daniel's shoulders whether or not he liked the person he spoke to.

Samuel Laidlaw got a smile, Daniel looking relaxed and pleased. They chatted for a goodly bit, then Daniel moved on, his shoulders going stiff as a board as the Barstows approached. Michael did not blame him. He had associated with Madeline out of desperation when he first arrived in Virginia, and, indeed, habit. She was the sort of person he was accustomed to.

More and more he found he disliked the kind of people he had been accustomed to in his former life.

He was greeted warmly by the Pastor, his hand pumped within an inch of its life.

"Michael St. James. What an unexpected pleasure!"

"Now, Pastor Lawrence, I have been to church many times since I arrived."

"Yes, yes, of course. I simply assumed this Eve you would be out…"

"Carousing?" He hid a smile. "My ability to do so is compromised by the lack of appropriate opportunity, sir."

"Yes. How lucky we are to live in such a virtuous parish."

"Oh, yes." He did not bat an eye, not even when Daniel looked over the diminutive Widow Harriston's head and waggled an eyebrow at him. Damn the man, anyway. "I'm certain that's why my father sent me here, hmmm? To get me away from all bad influences."

"A wise man indeed. Happy Christmas to you, Brother St. James." The preacher clapped him on the shoulder.

"And to you, sir."

The better part of an hour elapsed before he could escape, and his ears rang with genuine expressions of goodwill, even from those who did not care for his ways. There was something about Christmas that warmed even the coldest of men.

He knew it would be some time before Daniel joined him, so Michael rode home slowly, savoring the muffled, bright world of snow that was the road between his home and town. The whole world was peace, and the stars shone brightly, and for a moment he could fancy how a wise man felt.

But only for a moment, for he had never been wise.

Elias awaited him when he returned home, taking his coat and pushing him in to warm up by the fire.

"Everything is as you asked, sir."

"Excellent. Except there is one thing I asked you to do that you have not," he returned.

Elias raised one brow, face creasing in a frown. "What is that, sir?"

"Take the rest of the night and all of tomorrow for yourself. And tell Cook and the stable hands to as well, save for the morning feeding."

A wide smile broke out on Elias' stolid face. "Yes, sir. Thank you, sir."

"You're welcome, Elias. Happy Christmas."

Elias clumped off, leaving Michael nothing but the crackle of the fire and the ticking of the grand hall clock to keep him company while he awaited his guest. Daniel. A guest. The thought was laughable now.

Daniel had become the very center of his world.

He stripped off his coat and cravat, carefully placing the jeweled cravat pin aside so he would not lose it. He only had so many such items left, and he could not be cavalier with them. Then he put on the dressing gown Elias had left out for him and settled with a book, awaiting Daniel's knock upon his door.

His concentration was poor, however, thinking

upon how Daniel had come to mean so much to him. Really, it quite terrified him. He had never met anyone he could not walk away from, and yet it was almost a relief his father was not ready to call him home, for then he was not forced to decide between them.

The knock on the door startled him out of a light doze. Michael rose and answered it, smiling as he opened the door and let Daniel in.

"I began to fear you would not come."

"Took me a damnably long time to extricate myself. I hope you are pleased I did so just for you."

"Ha." Michael played valet, taking Daniel's coat. "Even were I not awaiting you, you would have run as fast as you could as soon as you could."

"Yes, but 'tis much more pleasant to have you to run to."

Moving close, Daniel put hands on him, and Michael closed his eyes, enjoying that first sublime thrill he got from Daniel touching him, relishing the shiver that went up his spine. The rough growth of Daniel's beard scrubbed his cheek as they kissed, leaving a tingle in its wake, making him gasp.

"I am glad you came. Happy Christmas, Daniel."

"And to you, St. James."

They smiled at each other like the fools they were, and Michael tugged at Daniel's hand. "Come, let us in by the fire. I have a gift for you."

"You needn't give me things." But a pleased smile lit Daniel's face, and a flush rose in his cheeks, showing Daniel's pleasure in the very thought. Michael thought it entirely possible that few people had ever given to this man freely, depending on him instead to be the giver.

"Yes, well. It's naught but a trifle, but it is heartfelt nonetheless."

He went to the escritoire and pulled out a small parcel wrapped in ribbon. Turning it over and over in his hands, he took it to Daniel and handed it over.

"As I said, it is not much…"

Daniel looked as if he had given him the moon. The ribbons fell to the floor, and Daniel smiled over the trinket inside, a wax seal with his monogram on it.

"I noticed the one time you sent me a missive, Calhoun, that you were sadly lacking the accoutrements of fine correspondence."

"Yes, well, not all of us have your rarified tastes."

The look in Daniel's eye was almost frightening, evil as it was. The glint there gave Michael pause, making him think he ought to run. He stood his ground, though, as Daniel advanced, crossing his arms and planting his feet.

"What are you about, Calhoun?"

"Oh, I think I should like to try out my new seal."

Michael backed up a step, then two, as Daniel nearly bowled him over. In fact, Daniel kept on until he was pressed up against the escritoire.

"There is wax in the desk."

"Of course there is. Get it for me."

Turning, he pulled out a small wick of red sealing wax, handing it over. Daniel nodded, a satisfied sound coming from him. "Excellent. Now strip."

"I beg your pardon?" Goodness, he sounded like a prude, or perhaps a blushing virgin, of which he was neither. Still, Daniel's bald command took him utterly aback, and Michael stared.

"I said undress. Remove your clothing, St. James. Surely you have not forgotten how." Daniel sounded so commanding, and Michael thought he had taught the damned man too well how to play the games one played in the bedroom.

Well, of course he had not forgotten how to undress. Michael pulled off his robe, his shirt and trousers, stepping free of his stockings. He could not help but tease.

"So now what will you do with me?"

"Oh. Michael." The throaty growl that was Daniel's voice reminded him of nothing so much as a puma he had seen once in a traveling show, pure predator. One large, rough hand slid down his side, landing upon his hip, turning him to face the desk. The other hand he saw reach past him, taking up a candle. "The things I intend to do to you are myriad and best shown not spoken."

Hot wax landed upon the skin of his lower back, and Michael jumped and gasped. "Daniel?"

"Do not move, St. James. It will run."

He held his breath, held still, even as more wax dribbled against his skin, the tiny burn more a pleasure than a pain. The wax pooled at the small of his back, just above the crease of his buttocks, and he felt Daniel breathing on it, cooling it a bit. The sensation teased his senses, made him rise up on his toes to get more.

Then something firm and cold pressed into the wax, marking his skin, sealing it, and Daniel rose to speak low and dangerous next to his ear. "Mine."

"Oh." Oh, yes. Daniel had him, body and soul. Michael moaned, pushing back, thighs opening like those of the most practiced courtesan, needing Daniel's touch as his own gift of the season.

Daniel did not tease him any longer. Instead Daniel pressed against him, swollen prick sliding along under his balls, pushing against his. The wet tip of Daniel's cock slid against the underside of his own, and Michael groaned, head lolling as his body rocked and shook.

Panting breaths landed on his ear, moist and hot, and Daniel rocked as well, moving against him, hipbones biting into Michael's arse. Michael, in turn, sang Daniel's name with more gusto than he had any holiday hymn, his voice rising on high with pleasure as Daniel reached about with one wax-dotted hand and cupped Michael's prick, stroking it in rough time.

They came together and pulled apart, and

Michael only wished they were actually joined, but this was good, and right, and it would do nicely. He spread even more, arching his back to get more of Daniel along his skin, and Daniel groaned, biting down on his shoulder. Michael grunted, barely holding himself in, and when Daniel used the hand not on his prick to reach between them and press on the wax seal, Michael let loose, spending so hard he saw stars on his closed eyelids.

"Michael!" Daniel's heat and wetness splashed against his thighs, Daniel's hands tightened on his skin until it was almost painful, and Michael could not think of a better way to spend Christmas Eve than this.

"Honestly, Jane, I think it's best if I don't." Daniel refused to reach for the babe Jane kept trying to foist off upon him. While Henry was hardly a tiny infant any longer, he was still quite small and Daniel felt he might break something if he held the wee thing.

Jane sighed. "Foals, kids, lambs… anything but a human child and you adore it. It's Christmas, Daniel. Hold your cousin for me while I check with Cook!"

Daniel rolled his eyes. "I don't—"

"Oh, for Heaven's sake." Michael joined them, bowing his head to Jane. "I'll hold him." He reached for Henry, who went to Michael easily, gurgling, his little hands grasping Michael's waistcoat. "Thank you for inviting me today, Madame."

"You look most comfortable holding him," Jane replied. "I must go and look in on the goose."

"He is in safe hands," Michael assured her.

Daniel glared at Michael once Jane had left them. "Must you make me look bad?"

Michael chuckled, then began making faces to amuse Henry. "I suppose he likes my fine feathers. Babies are distracted by frippery rather than substance."

"Ha." Daniel deserved the jibe, he supposed. He watched Henry, whose eyes were hazel like his mother's. The youngling was rather adorable. Michael didn't seem to have a bit of worry about the smallness of that fragile body, bouncing Henry with one hand. "I have not had much experience with children."

"My sister has a brood," Michael said, and a shadow made those golden eyes go dark.

"You miss them," Daniel said. He rarely thought about the life Michael had been forced to leave behind, and family seemed incongruous with the Michael he'd first met.

"Fat lot of good it does me," Michael said, his tone wry. "Most of the children won't even remember me soon, young as they are."

"I'm sorry." Daniel reached out to touch Michael's arm.

"Daniel! There you—" One of his older cousins, Letitia, stopped short a few paces away, staring between him and Michael. "Did I interrupt?"

"Not at all," Michael said. "We were keeping Henry company until Jane's return. Shall I take him to Gerard?" Michael gave them both a cheerful smile before leaving him alone with his plump, cheerful relation.

"Happy Christmas, Letitia."

"And to you! I wanted to ask if you might take Peter to the livestock auction when it resumes in February."

Peter was Letitia's second husband, the first having died of a bad heart in his middle years. Daniel rather liked the man.

"Naturally. He only needs to tell me what he's looking for."

A slight frown marred her forehead, even as she nodded. "Mr. St. James. You have become friends with him?"

Daniel worked to stay relaxed, to keep the smile upon his face. "I have."

"Ah. Is that precisely wise, Daniel?"

He did stiffen at her careful tone. "Why do you ask?"

"Well, I know that you and Jane rarely deal with society outside of our parish, but he comes from a well-known family. He's something of a pariah with them, you know."

"No. Or rather, I know his father banished him for some perceived ill."

"Dueling." Letitia leaned closer, whispering. "He nearly killed a man in a duel. His moral fiber—"

Daniel took her hand from his arm. "Now, cousin, you know I judge a man by how he treats me. I thought him all frippery to begin with, too, but he treats his horses well, and he is unfailingly kind to Jane."

"But."

"Not another word. Tell Peter he is welcome anytime."

She gave him a tremulous smile. "Very well. Thank you."

"Let us go find something to drink, hmm?" Daniel presented a crooked elbow, the truce offered and accepted when she rested her fingers on his sleeve.

He had made judgements against Michael to begin with it was true, but he would not hear it now. Not one bit. He'd made his choice and not even his family would convince Daniel he was mistaken.

Michael stood in front of the cheval glass, attempting to tie his cravat in the newest style. His mother had sent him etchings from the Boston news rags, and fashion had changed significantly since he'd left.

Not that he cared, particularly, but he was supposed to, and it would look odd if he did not try to keep up. Really, what better time was there to show off a new look than at a New Year's Eve soiree?

He could hear Daniel behind him, rummaging through something, and he was very afraid he did not want to look. He glanced in the mirror and sighed. Especially if Daniel was clothed.

"You know, St. James, I cannot recall ever seeing you wear these."

Arching one brow in a manner he knew Daniel abhorred, Michael turned to see what the other man was talking about. Which caused him to frown, surprised, as Calhoun so often made him do. "That would be because I don't wear them. They belonged to my mother."

Placing the triple-strand pearl choker back into Michael's jewel box, Daniel continued to search. "I thought your mother was still alive. And did you not say you have a sister? I can hardly see you inheriting them instead of she."

"I did not inherit them. My mother gave them to me when my father sent me here. She thought perhaps I might sell them if I encountered difficult circumstances. I suppose I ought to post them back to her. They are becoming dull from disuse."

"How's that?"

"What are you looking for?"

"Cravat pin. I seem to have lost mine. What about the pearls?"

Rolling his eyes, Michael moved to stand next

to Daniel, easily finding a cravat pin in the chaos he'd created. "Pearls lose their luster when they are not frequently worn against the skin. 'Tis a proven thing. These are becoming somewhat lifeless. And since I cannot imagine finding myself in any kind of desperate situation, now that I have you, I should return them to mother."

Daniel turned to him and smiled, a wicked gleam in his eyes. "Are you saying you expect me to support you monetarily if your good fortune should falter?"

"Why, certainly."

"And what do I get in return?"

"Sexual favors. The benefit of my wide variety of experience and expertise."

"Bounder."

"Indubitably." Fingering the pearls, Michael looked speculatively at Daniel.

"What?"

"I would hate to send these back to my dear mother without conditioning them first."

"And just how do you propose to do that?"

"Prolonged contact with someone's skin."

"Michael!" Daniel sounded as scandalized as he looked. "You cannot be serious. They belong to your mother."

Wrapping the pearls into his closed fist, Michael raised them to his face and stroked them over his lips. "Right now they belong to me. Surely you do not want them to lose their value. Just in case you cast me out and I must support myself."

"Absolutely not, St. James." Daniel's eyes belied his denial by focusing on the pearls where they rested against Michael's mouth. His eyes, usually a rich, mossy color, turned a clear, hot green the way they did when he was truly aroused. The thought intrigued him, no doubt, but as the resident puritan, he must protest. This was one of Michael's favorite games. He advanced, Daniel retreated. Which forced Michael to play his trump card.

"Of course, if you would rather go to Jane's party straight on and listen to Widow Sutton's charming litany of complaints about her gout while her stultifying daughter clings to your arm and flashes her bony cleavage, then by all means, let us put the pearls away."

Calhoun gaped at him. "You. You were the one who said we must arrive early. I would much rather. Oh, why am I arguing?" The cravat pin fell back into the jewel box with a tiny plink, and Daniel began to work at removing his messy neckcloth. "Which patch of skin did you have in mind?"

God above, but Daniel was never so attractive to Michael as when he put aside his discomfiture and played the wanton. Pretending to consider, Michael tilted his head to the side and enjoyed the sight of Daniel's fine lawn shirt sliding off wide shoulders and down well-muscled arms. "I shall have to see it all to make a decision, I think."

Stripping out of his breeches and hose, Daniel

stood nude before Michael, one hip cocked forward, hands out at his sides. "Look your fill, then."

Look he did, greedily. It seemed as though he never got enough of the sight of Daniel Calhoun. The well-defined musculature, so at odds with his station, the light covering of springy hair on his chest, a few shades darker than that on his head, the narrow hips and solid thighs, all conspired to make Michael short of breath. And the cock. That glorious, heavy cock with its delicate skin and prominent veins. That fairly made his mouth water.

"On the bed."

"Yes, sir," Daniel replied smartly, and turned to climb into the big bed they had made theirs. He sprawled there, open and inviting, a wide smile on his face as Michael tried to remove his own clothing and encountered the difficulty of the pearls he had completely forgotten. Unwinding them, Michael dropped them on the foot of the ticking and stripped as quickly as he could without taking his eyes from the veritable feast before him. Sophisticate that he was, experienced as he had become, the sight was enough to make him feel like a fifteen-year-old boy with his first chambermaid.

Perseverance finally won out, and the struggle with his attire ended. With a deep breath to calm himself somewhat, Michael picked up the pearls and dangled them from his hand, brushing them lightly over Daniel's toes. The toes twitched, as did the rest of the man they were attached to, and

Michael smiled. He dragged the strand over the decidedly undainty arch of Calhoun's foot, up to the inside of his knee, rubbing against the tender skin there. The pearls warmed to Daniel's body heat, and to Michael's, and he suddenly needed to feel Daniel's warmth against his flesh.

The bed dipped under his added weight, and a strangled sound came from Daniel's throat when Michael straddled his legs. Sensitized skin rubbed together, making them both gasp, and Michael leaned forward to brush the pearls against Daniel's cheek, admiring the contrast of their smooth luster to the stubbled roughness of his lover's face.

Rumbling, Daniel reached for him, and Michael drew back, batting away the searching hands. "Put your hands over your head," he instructed, and Daniel did, seemingly docile. His eyes promised retribution at some time in the future. The look was dark and sweet and burned in Michael's belly like good whiskey. He draped the pearls across Daniel's throat and let them rest there while he offered a kiss as compensation. The kiss began as something light and teasing but rapidly became voracious.

When Michael finally managed to break the contact, they both found it difficult to breathe. Determined to finish their game, Michael pulled Daniel's hands from his hair and pressed them up against the headboard once more. The pearls snaked down Daniel's chest, catching lightly against the hair there, wrapping around one nipple. The delicious sound Daniel made told he him should speed the course a bit, so he put his mouth to the nipple's neglected twin while rolling the glowing pearls along Daniel's belly and hips.

The taste was one he would never tire of, the tang of salt and lust and Daniel. He nipped harshly, and Daniel moaned, and the world spun dizzily on its axis. Michael was now the one on his back, looking up, and Daniel smiled down at him, triumphant. In the scuffle he'd lost hold of the pearls, and Daniel rubbed them against him. Here, and now here, slick with their sweat and warm, but still far cooler than Michael's burning skin. All along the trail of the necklace Daniel licked and kissed and bit until Michael knew he surely would go mad. When had his Daniel learned to tease so?

The feel of the jewels between his legs shocked him nearly senseless. Sliding down across his cock to his balls and back up to curl around him, a sleek, alien pressure. His mother's pearls! It was, perhaps, the most perverse thing Daniel had ever done, and it excited him unbearably. Michael arched into the foreign caress as it tightened, then loosened, again and again. The rough silk of Daniel's voice vibrated against the head of his cock, and the enormous drop pearl at the center of the choker nudged at the entrance to his body, and it was too much. His completion snapped his body into a taut arc, and the only understandable word he forced out was Daniel's name.

At some length he came back to himself to find Daniel regarding him with a smug expression. Dangling the necklace above them, Daniel assumed an appropriately sober mien. "I think you conditioned them."

"Well they don't call it pearly essence for nothing, I suppose," Michael returned.

Daniel nearly lost the fight to keep from laughing, if the quiver of his lips was any indication. The glint in his eye told the same story, but he won out. "Is this what you call handing out pearls of wisdom?"

"More like casting pearls before swine, I should think." And with that, neither of them was able to hold back their mirth, and they laughed together. And that was more precious to Michael than any strand of pearls.

The party was made infinitely better, Daniel supposed, by the fact that he was wearing Michael's cravat pin and he still had the scent of Michael's seed in his nose.

His cheeks heated. Good heavens, the things they did together. And he was turning into an utter wanton, throwing caution and good sense to the wind and playing with Michael like a man of low morals.

How he loved it.

The other guests bothered him not one whit; in fact, he mingled quite easily, feeling most buoyed by his and Michael's encounter. 'Twas astonishing, really. It was Samuel who finally caught him, pulling him aside by the sleeve.

"Daniel. You look like a cat licking cream. How are you?"

"Most well, Samuel. Most well." He clapped the other man on the shoulder. "Come and have a pipe with me?"

Samuel nodded. "I would like that. I have something I wish to speak to you about."

"Of course, of course." Whatever it was, it would not dampen his mood. Daniel automatically sought Michael with his eyes, finding him talking to a formidable old widow woman, barely avoiding her cane as it clomped about his feet.

He got his tobacco pouch and accompanied Samuel out of the ballroom, past the groaning buffet. They did not stop in the men's parlor, as he thought they might. Instead they went outside, into the chill night air of the verandah.

Daniel very deliberately stuffed his pipe and tamped and lighted it before turning to Samuel with polite curiosity. "Well, this certainly is a private word you wish to have."

"Yes it is, Daniel. You know damned well I hold you in great esteem, and nothing anyone says will change that."

"Why, thank you, Samuel." Daniel did not

snort, though he wished to. Such things prefaced with words such as those were always inflammatory gossip and well meant, but annoying as all Hell.

"But. Your reputation has suffered of late, Daniel. The company you keep has tongues wagging."

"What does not have their tongues wagging?"

He did not mean to be rude, dismissing Samuel out of hand, but he was angrier at his friends and neighbors for condemning Michael than he was at them for gossiping about him. Despite his earlier assertions that Michael was a ne'er do well.

"Daniel, some of the things they say…well, they could be ruinous." Samuel touched his arm again, this time pleadingly. "You should have a care. What you do is your own affair, but do not flaunt it so."

His appreciation for Samuel's steady friendship was in no way diminished by his annoyance at petty gossips, so Daniel smiled and nodded. "Very well, Samuel. I shall attempt to be more circumspect, even though hiding is not in my nature."

"I do know it," Samuel said, "but this could be the end of you, and I enjoy your company."

They puffed companionably until their pipes burnt down, and Daniel gave Samuel a short bow. "Shall we attend the auction together this Saturday, Samuel? I hear there's a mare that's a fine match to the yearling you bought some months ago."

"Oh, I say, an excellent notion, Calhoun. Excellent. I think we should."

"I will see you at the fork at the road at eight then."

They often met that way, and it would look well, he thought. Perhaps dispel some of the worst maligning.

"You shall indeed. Good night, Daniel."

"Good night."

They parted ways at the entry, and Daniel sailed back into the ballroom, head high and back straight. He would be damned if people who had never approved of him or had never made him feel welcome any road were going to make him feel guilty for finding his pleasure where he could.

Michael St. James was worth any amount of their displeasure.

"Well, do you think you have conquered him?"

"I beg your pardon?" Michael looked at Madeline Barstow down the entire length of his nose. Really, how had he ever found her more socially agreeable than someone like Jane or Daniel? He supposed he hadn't had a choice, had he? He'd never met anyone like his lover before.

"Mister Calhoun. Have you conquered him?"

She looked a fright in a sheer gown a la regina, her ribs showing in her chest, her own lank hair forced into a series of Medusa-like curls. In his more charitable moments, Michael felt sorry for her. This was not one of them.

"If you mean, Madeline dear, have we become friends, then yes. I suppose we have. Whatever else you imply I leave to your own conscience."

She pursed her lips, fanning herself furiously. "Oh, come, Michael. You have no need to dissemble with me. I know very well what sort of man you are. I heard about you before you ever arrived in Richmond, and I saw how you cut a swath there. I understand you."

"Perhaps you do at that. But I vow you have no idea what sort of man *he* is."

With that he moved away, feeling her presence like a cloying fog of ill will. God, what had possessed him all these years to move in such circles? He turned about the ballroom once, watching Daniel with what he feared was ill-concealed hunger, and finally settled on getting some of Jane's plain but wonderful feast. He heard complaints from some, praises from others, and wondered why some people chose to come to Jane and Gerard's affairs if they thought them so coarse and uncouth.

"There you are. Fill me a plate, will you, Michael?"

Since he had already spoken to Jane several times during the evening, her pleasantly surprised look must be patently false. Michael raised a brow at her, just as he would at Daniel, and saw her scowl, just as Daniel would. Michael hid a smile.

"What would you like, my dear lady?"

"One of everything. Then we must sit together and talk."

Oh, dear. He nodded, loading two plates with an obscene amount of food; two could play her game. He then motioned her to precede him and find them a seat.

"Would you not prefer to eat with Gerard?"

"He has taken himself off to the men's parlor. Be pleasant, Michael, or I shall hurt you."

"Yes, madam."

They sat together, and he handed her a plate. He noticed she had chosen a secluded alcove where it would be difficult for one to eavesdrop.

"Now, what are you about, Jane?"

"I wish to talk to you about Daniel." She looked at him, hazel eyes bright and serious, her mouth set in a determined line.

"I have not hurt him."

"I know." She sighed, nibbling a piece of lamb. "But, Michael, the two of you are being reckless. It is becoming quite obvious to some other than me that you are involved. You should know most people do not hold with that sort of behavior, Michael. Surely this cannot be all that different, even in New York or Philadelphia."

"It is generally frowned upon, yes." The back of his neck positively itched, and Michael rubbed at it. "I am not out to ruin him, Jane."

The lines in her forehead softened. "I know that, Michael. In fact, I think you have come to care for him very much."

"I adore him." It was a bald truth, and he said it with all of the conviction of his heart.

"Then you must have a care." Leaning near, she put a hand on his knee. "I do not ask you to forbear. Frankly, I wish anyone who can find happiness in whatever way they can the best of luck. And you make him happy, Michael. I have never seen him smile so."

A flush of pleasure lit him from the inside at those words. "Thank you, Jane. If you feel we are being careless, I shall endeavor to be more circumspect. I promise you."

"Thank you." Her smile reminded him of Daniel's, wide and true and making her eyes sparkle.

He patted her hand. "Now eat, because you are still feeding two."

A fine blush rose in her cheeks. "Yes, yes. I swear, you men."

She ate, though, and heartily, not the dainty nibbles of a society woman. He was pleased. She needed her strength. Eventually Gerard returned, reeking of some sort of local tobacco smoke, and Michael left Jane to his tender mercies.

He needed to talk to Daniel.

He found Daniel sitting on a bench in the deserted dining room, booted feet crossed at the ankle, head resting against the flocked wallpaper. Michael sat next to him, crossing one ankle over the opposite knee.

"Are we indiscreet?" he asked without preamble.

Daniel snorted. "For tidewater Virginia? Of course we are, you nitwit."

"Then…" Michael stared. He was not at all sure what to say. "Should we no longer see so much of one another? I would not cause you difficulty, Daniel."

"You confound me every day, Michael. Why should you be any different in this?"

"Daniel, I…"

"No." Daniel turned to face him, sitting up with his hands braced on his knees. "I will not give you up. Not for these fools who have never known nor have cared to know me. Once I have set my mind upon something, I make sure I have it, St. James. I have set my mind on you."

Oh. There was no way to hide the effect Daniel's words had on him, so he covered himself with one hand, just in case someone should walk out and find them so. He smiled, pleased beyond words.

Daniel simply smiled back, eyes such a clear green that Michael knew instantly what Daniel was thinking. He pretended to be scandalized. "Calhoun! It is your cousin's house."

"And where better? I know where the private rooms are abovestairs." Standing, tall and imposing and utterly his, Daniel held out a hand to help him up. "Come, St. James. Let us see how indiscreet we might be. I have an urge to ring in the New Year as I intend to carry on all the rest of the months. Shall we?"

"Yes." He took that hand without hesitation, following Daniel to the servant's stairs. "Let's."

Chapter Seven

Richmond suited Daniel not at all. Too much noise, too many people, too much…of everything. And not enough of Michael St. James. Daniel missed the man deeply, like a sharp pain in his gut.

He tipped his hat as he stepped aside, letting a tiny, round lady pass, narrowly avoiding the spoke of her parasol as it practically decapitated him. Damnation. He wanted to roar. Instead, he went to the land office and did his business, registering yet another plot of his land with Jane, in trust for her new child.

At one time he had thought perhaps he would marry, have heirs of his own. Now, though, he knew better. He would not marry, not after this affair with St. James. It would be dishonest and unfair to any poor female who tied up to his wagon. Perhaps a few short months were too few to make such a decision, but there it was. A week previously he had decided to start the process of making sure that if something happened to him, his hard-won working farm would go to Jane's capable management. He needed it to be taken care of.

Oh, it had lifted a few brows. It would, of course, do so, as he put it in little Henry's name but made Jane the regent of it should something happen to him before Henry was of age.

"Are you certain?" asked James Drury, the distinguished old gentleman working at the land office. "I see your cousin is married."

"She is. Gerard is a lovely man, but quite the nincompoop. He will run the land into the ground." No, he would not deed anything directly to Gerard, as much as Daniel liked the fellow.

"Yes, well." Gray eyebrows gyrated. "A woman owning property."

Daniel scowled at the man. "She will not own it. Her son will. I expect she will teach him how to tend it."

"I—well, as you wish." There was much stamping and sealing and huffing, but the deed was done.

When he stepped out of the office for the last time and made his way to the inn, it was raining. Naturally. Wet and cold, and utterly gray, the day made him miss home and hearth even more, and Daniel pulled his coat about him, walking faster.

"Daniel!" Someone hailed. "Daniel Calhoun?"

"Damnation." Daniel tied not to snarl when he turned about to see who was calling his name. Ah, Edward Jennings, and old friend from the county.

"Good to see you, Daniel!" Edward said, reaching out to pump his hands. "What brings you to Richmond?"

"Business," Daniel said shortly, then sighed at Edward's surprised expression. "This damnable weather has fouled my mood. Let me buy you a drink and make it up to you."

Edward clapped him on the back. "I'll take you up on it, Daniel. You must tell me all the news from home."

"Indeed." Daniel kept his new smile in place, trying to be kind when all he wanted to do was pack his bag and leave this squalid place behind. He would talk to Edward and then he would run before anyone else thought to keep him from his goal.

He was determined to get home. And to let Michael St. James work his magic and take the chill right off.

The day was perfectly dank and dreary. What Virginia lacked in temperate summers, being vilely hot and humid, it made up in rainy, mud-splattered winters. In short, the climate suited Michael St. James not at all.

Standing in the entry of his home there, Michael waited for Elias to bring his horse around, all the while debating whether or not, in fact, he even

130

wished to go for a ride in this rancid weather. Gray ranged as far as the eye could see, with a sullen drizzle falling upon already soggy ground. The only thing encouraging him to leave home and hearth was the fact that his stallion had not been exercised in two days, and Michael did not wish to inflict this infernal rain on a poor, unsuspecting groom. Not when the horse was likely in as foul a mood as Michael himself.

Damnation, but he missed Calhoun. Missed the solid weight of the man in his bed at night. Even more, he missed the simple companionship. Without his farming duties keeping him occupied as they did in the other seasons, Daniel had time to share of his company, and they now grudgingly admitted they had a great deal in common. Quite frankly, it was the only thing that made his continued exile bearable.

Which, he supposed, was why he was so edgy of late. So much so that his usually affable servants avoided him. With Daniel in Richmond, attending business there for his family, and being gone well over a fortnight, Michael was, quite simply, lonely. And randy. Terribly, terribly randy.

Slapping his gloves impatiently against his knee, Michael waited a seemingly unending amount of time before he heard the ring of shod hooves in the courtyard. Finally. The butler had long since left him to his own devices, so Michael was on the way to open the door himself when it burst open, nearly bowling him over.

"Elias! What the devil do you mean..."

"Shut up, St. James, and welcome me home."

There was only enough time for Michael to register Daniel's voice before he was enveloped in a damp embrace that smelled of wet wool and horses, tobacco smoke, and earthy, male musk. And oh, Calhoun kissed him, deep and breath-stealing, rough beard stubble abrading his face. It was marvelous, and before Michael could take in air to tell Calhoun it was about time, he was backed into one side of the foyer and the bottom stair riser hit his heels.

Teetering, Michael yelped, and Daniel held him up with strong arms, allowing him to regain his balance. Once he stopped his backward descent, Daniel let go of him just long enough to shed his many-caped great coat and toss it down upon the stairs. The man yanked at Michael's coat as well, and, bemused, Michael gave it up, only to have it thrown unceremoniously atop Daniel's. "Now see here, Calhoun," he began, but Daniel gave him a push, and he landed with a thump somewhere around the third stair up, putting a sizeable dent in his spine.

"I said shut up," Daniel repeated, and he pushed Michael's legs apart, settling between them and kissing him again. The kiss stirred Michael unbearably, as did the strong hand that settled upon the placket of his breeches, rubbing and kneading at the stiffened flesh there. Daniel was a mature, confident man, but he rarely took the initiative in their lovemaking, which Michael knew to be a symptom of his inexperience in being with other men. Therefore, this aggression on Daniel's part was a heady thing, leaving Michael aching and breathless. Pressing against him, Daniel kissed and licked at his lips, and Michael opened to him eagerly, arching into the hand that held him so warmly.

A deep, rough sound tore from Daniel's chest and he pulled back, leaving Michael reaching for him. He slapped Michael's hands away and efficiently opened the many daunting layers of their clothing just enough to feel skin upon skin before pressing back down against him. Did that needy, throbbing sound come from his own throat? It must have, and Daniel bit into the juncture of his neck and jaw, sliding along his entire body. The springy hair on Daniel's chest teased his nipples unmercifully, and the slide of hot flesh where their opened breeches met almost undid him.

"Missed this. Missed you." The words were gasped against his collarbone, and then Daniel was wrapping his hot lips around Michael's nipple while those big workingman's fingers danced along his cock, and even the sharp edge of the step under his ribs disappeared in favor of the sensation. Warm and wet, Daniel's tongue traced down over his belly and hips, until his cock bumped against Daniel's chin and then those lips were wrapping around the head and sucking strongly, and it took every ounce of self-possession in Michael's screaming body to keep him from climaxing right then and there. Never had Daniel willingly tasted him this way; he had always been reticent about it, emphatically so. Now, however, he proved without a doubt that he had paid attention all of the times Michael had done it to him, using lips and tongue and just a hint of teeth, because Michael liked it rough and ready.

One huge hand cradled his balls and squeezed ever so gently while the lips around him tightened and took him in as deeply as they could, and Michael could hold back no longer. With a loud, breathless cry, he emptied himself into Daniel's voracious mouth, seeing stars when his head banged against the solid wood beneath it. The pleasure was almost unbearable.

For long minutes afterward, Daniel rested with his face against Michael's thigh, and Michael curled his fingers into Daniel's unruly hair and stroked. When Daniel finally moved, it was to lay alongside him, one arm sliding under Michael to cushion his back from the stairs. Reaching languidly for Daniel's opened fly, Michael encountered a sticky wetness that could not be his own, and Daniel chuckled, a light breath against his lips.

"There's no need, St. James. I fear I have already spent myself."

"Well, then, we shall simply have to fill you back up. But upstairs, if you please. I'm too old to be rolling about on the floor." Sobering, Michael kissed Daniel deeply, tasting the salty bitterness of his own release. "You were gone too long."

"I was. Next time you'll come with me."

"You may depend upon it."

The sound of a throat clearing made them both start, and Michael looked down into the atrium to see his man Elias, studiously peering at the ceiling, a blush staining his cheeks. "I take it, Mr. Michael, that you will not be needing your afternoon ride?"

"No, thank you, Elias. It appears I've already had one."

"I think I may have asked, St. James. But are you sure your man Elias is discreet?"

"I would trust him with my life, Daniel. You need not worry he will talk out of turn."

Daniel nodded, unwilling to move any more than that. They lay in Michael's big bed, the down ticking soft beneath them, the heavy quilts atop them and the crackling fire on the hearth keeping them warm. Michael rested atop him, and he stroked the long line of Michael's spine, down to the curve of one buttock.

Such a wondrous thing, Michael's body. So well formed. So strong. Oh, St. James had not his own brute strength, but he had a lean musculature than Daniel admired and an altogether pleasing arrangement of features. It was almost enough to make him forget his own impetuousness of putting his mouth to Michael's flesh in the foyer.

Almost.

He laughed wryly. "I simply fear that goes beyond what we can consider circumspect, Michael. And I did recently promise to be so."

"As did I." Those whiskey eyes peered up at him, Michael blinking slow and sleepily. "Jane?"

"Samuel Laidlaw."

"Ah. Indeed."

"And you? Jane?" He could just see Jane accosting Michael about it.

"Yes. She was most insistent that we cool our heels in public. But Elias is more of a friend than a servant, I assure you."

He had noticed, and admired, that relationship between servant and employer some time ago. The man he had once thought St. James to be could never lower himself to be friends with a valet-cum-butler. Daniel merely nodded again, his touches becoming more suggestive.

"What of Laidlaw, Daniel? Do you confide in him? Will he keep your secrets?"

"He will. I do not confide in him so much as trust him enough not to deny it. He knows, and he does not condemn me. It is as much as I can ask."

"Yes, I suppose it is." Michael kissed him, just a sweet, light brush of lips. "I am glad to know you have someone you may trust. It seems so many here would just as soon see you fall from grace, and I, well, they would love to see me falter."

"Of course they would. It is the way of people. If you do not agree with their motives or morals, they denounce you." Daniel laughed. "Look at how I thought of you until you convinced me otherwise."

"You still see me as a bounder and a cad."

"Of course I do." Pulling Michael more firmly atop him, Daniel squeezed the firm muscle under his hand, thumb dipping to trace Michael's crease. "Yet I have learned to admire the man beneath that fine façade."

"I think perhaps that is the kindest thing you have ever said to me."

Daniel would swear a flush rose in Michael's cheeks that owed nothing to his physical ministrations and all to his words, but he could be mistaken. The next kiss he received, however, owed much more to enthusiasm than to lazy happiness, so much that it made his lips tingle.

They kissed until they were breathless, until they rubbed and rocked and simply needed too hotly to back away. Michael touched him, fingers stroking down his chest to pinch and pull at his nipples, and he in turn pressed his fingers against the shadowed entry to Michael's body, pushing one inside easily. How quickly he had gotten past his assumed distaste for such things.

Michael moaned, his body sliding against

Daniel's restlessly, and Daniel pressed harder, his finger slipping in and out. So hot on the inside. So tight. Michael continually amazed and delighted him. Had someone told him he would fall so much in…well. Daniel shook off the thought and bit down on the jointure of Michael's neck and shoulder.

"Calhoun, Daniel. Please."

"Yes? What would you have of me, St. James?"

"I would have you in me."

Michael rolled away from him, stretching out on the bed, looking as enticing as he ever had. Daniel rolled to his side, tracing the lines of Michael's body.

"Can we not do what we did before?"

"No. I want it this way. Come, you will not hurt me. The oil is by the bed."

Daniel was not certain about this at all. Every time before if he had entered Michael it was with Michael above him, controlling the penetration. He honestly feared what would happen if he were expected to keep from harming Michael on his own.

He pulled back, uncertain and hating it. "I do not think…"

"You cannot think about this, my dear. You must do it. Come, please."

The hand Michael held out to him had less to do with his capitulation than the pleading expression on Michael's face. Damnation. How was a man to be expected to deny that?

He took Michael's hand and came down atop him, Michael opening his legs to let Daniel settle between them. He felt enveloped by Michael's warmth, his need. His prick pressed against Michael's thigh as he leaned to reach the oil Michael now kept beside the bed. He had protested the decadence; Michael had argued for its practicality.

The oil spilled as his hands shook, and Daniel cursed himself silently as a fool. It was not as if they'd not done this before. It was just upside down.

Finally he got his fingers coated and put two against Michael's opening. One slid in to the first knuckle, Michael still so tight every time he tested him, and Daniel went with that, slipping it deeper while Michael moaned and thrashed like the wanton he was.

The second slid in after he got Michael stretched somewhat, and that was all of the preparation he was allowed as Michael rose up, grabbing the oil and spilling a generous amount down over his prick.

"Now, Daniel. Stop dithering."

He scowled. "I do not dither, St. James."

"Of course not." Those whiskey eyes danced as Michael laughed at him. "Inside me, if you please."

"I please."

Daniel pulled his fingers free and pressed the head of his prick against Michael's opening. He slid inside so easily, like it was meant to be that way, like they belonged joined. Betimes it scared him, made him fear what would happen should Michael take it into his head to leave. He would someday. Daniel knew he would. He would have to go back to his life of indolent luxury.

He sighed, and Michael reached up to touch his face, smoothing the lines there.

"What makes you frown so, Calhoun?"

"Nothing." Kissing Michael's palm, he began to move. "Nothing at all."

"Liar." Yet Michael smiled at him, eyes aglow, stroking his cheek and throat before pulling him down for a fierce kiss, and for a time, it was all forgotten. All but the feel of Michael around him, under him. Pressing down with his hips, he rocked, his breath huffing from him as he tried to hang on to his control, tried to adjust the depth of his penetration.

Michael did not let him. There was no holding back. None. Lean, muscled legs wrapped around him, and Michael's hands flattened on his arse, pulling him down harder, faster, more. What could he do but give in to the demand? Daniel thrust, his back bowing, his thighs straining, pushing his prick into Michael's willing body over and over, sharp cries bursting from his throat.

A soft grunt was all of the warning Daniel received before Michael squeezed down on him so hard he saw stars, and the wet heat of Michael's seed burst out onto Daniel's skin. Daniel cried out, his own tiny death taking him quite out of himself, his seed spilling into Michael, filling him deep.

They rested together, the quilt pulled up on them again, Daniel slipping off to one side and curling close to Michael, arm resting low on Michael's belly.

"That was most unrestrained. Not circumspect at all."

Michael nodded solemnly. "Yes. But we were not in public."

Daniel smiled, and Michael chuckled, and suddenly they were laughing together, hard enough that the bed shook beneath them.

"Yes," he said finally. "Thank God for that."

"So, do you wish to attend the Squire Madden's ball?" Michael drew idle patterns on Daniel's skin, enjoying the glow of firelight on it. The winter was not ready to give way to spring, but the chill was off enough that with a blazing fire he could push the coverlet back without Daniel protesting vociferously.

"I suppose I must. Gerard will be in Richmond, so Jane has reserved my escort."

"Ah." Michael did not let the sigh that rose to his lips escape. How he loathed having to attend these affairs separately. Not that there was any way they could attend them together, was there? Society was what it was. There was no place for two men together in it, and there never would be, he imagined.

"Ah? Are you feeling the sting of it too?"

"Hmm?" Rising up on one elbow, Michael looked down at Daniel's face, smiling at the thoroughly disgruntled look he found there. "I believe I am, yes."

"I vow, St. James. They must create these unfortunate affairs to torture us."

"Oh, yes, they set out to think of ways to amuse themselves at our expense. Most of them would never give us a second thought, Daniel, and be glad for it."

"I am. Believe me. Still, it would be..."

"Yes."

Michael stayed where he was only a moment before rolling out of bed, too restless to lie still. He wandered to his dressing room, looking for his dressing gown, not really wanting to go back out into the bedroom. He heard floorboards creak as Daniel came to him, felt the warmth of Daniel's body as the man closed strong arms about him.

"What is it?"

Michael turned, closing his arms about Daniel in answer, head resting on Daniel's broad chest. He heard the thump of Daniel's heart, and it soothed him.

"Let's run away together," he said.

"What?" The heartbeat he listened to jumped, starting a hard pounding. "What nonsense do you speak now, St. James? This is my home."

"Yes, but we could go somewhere, anywhere. Together. We could find a place out with the savages and love one another as we wish."

"Don't be absurd, Michael. There's nowhere safe for that, and I have far too many obligations to simply up and run. Even for you."

Something broke inside him, just a little. Michael nodded. "I know. I was only teasing you, Calhoun. I know how much your land and your family mean to you."

"You should not tease about such things, St. James." Daniel tilted his head up, looked him in the eye, Daniel's eyes sober as a churchgoer's on Easter. "This place means everything to me. I have built it with my own hands. I could not conceive leaving it. 'Tis bad enough I know now I will not have heirs to tend it."

"Will not have…" Michael stared. "I assume you blame this on me."

"There is no blame, Michael." Daniel let him go, rolling up and beginning to pace back and forth once his feet hit the floor. "There is only the knowledge that I would be lying to any woman I ever married about my proclivities, and I refuse to do that."

"Your proclivities. How provincial." He could not help but assume the brittle mantle of his old, ironic ways, his voice sounding offensive even to his own ears. "You need foster no guilt over me,

Calhoun. I seduced you, if you recall."

"And I allowed it. How hypocritical would it be of me to saddle a woman with…"

"With what?" Michael stepped in front of Daniel, so close that the hair on Michael's chest brushed his nipples. "With a catamite? With a sodomite who is so filthy he cannot touch anything and have it remain clean? It is lovely to know how you really think of me and what we have found here, Daniel. Really."

Daniel flinched, reached out to touch his shoulder. Michael shrugged it off, and they stared at one another for long moments, silent and still. Daniel broke first.

"That is not what I think of *you*, Michael."

"No. It is only what you think of yourself, thanks to me."

He desperately wanted Daniel to deny it. He waited, watched that beloved face for any sign he was wrong, but all he saw was an agony of guilt.

"Get out."

Daniel started, shaking himself visibly and moving to touch him again. Michael backed up, practically tripping over the small chair he used when assuming his boots.

"No, Daniel. Get out of my house and do not come back. I will not be the cause of your self-flagellation. I have no intention of being blamed for your ruin. Out."

"St. James. Michael. Please...I didn't mean."

"Yes, you did. Damnation, I said get out!"

He turned his back, crossing his arms over his chest. There was no way he could force Daniel out physically. Unless. Yes. He heard Daniel move behind him, not away, but toward him, and Michael lunged for the case that held his dueling pistols, pulling one out with a quickness that belied his shaking hands. He turned on Daniel in a heartbeat, ruthlessly ignoring the shock on Daniel's face.

"Out, damn your eyes."

"Michael! Where did you get those?" Daniel actually looked worried, as if Michael would actually shoot him.

"They were another gift. This time from my father. Ironic, isn't it that using them got me banished? I never miss. Now get out."

Daniel backed away this time, stopping to retrieve his clothes and dress hastily, never taking his eyes off the bore of the pistol. When Daniel had finished dressing he tried one more time, eyes gone clear, just as they did when they made love.

"Michael, I only want to say something."

His resolve wavered, but his aim never did. "No. Just leave, if you please."

"I do not. But I will because you insist. We will revisit this, St. James. You may depend upon it."

Daniel left him in a flurry of stamping and muttering. Michael did not let down his guard until he heard the exterior door slam. Then he put the pistol away and slumped down into the chair he'd almost broken a leg over only moments before.

Surely Daniel Calhoun would be the death of him. He laughed, the sound harsh, almost a sob. His father would approve. Daniel would break his heart, and that was a fitting punishment for the man he had been, leaving broken hearts in his wake without even a second thought.

They did say the punishment should fit the crimes, after all.

Chapter Eight

Daniel Calhoun was miserable. So miserable, in fact, he was like a bear with a wounded paw, and all and sundry of his acquaintance were avoiding him. He could not blame them.

Michael would not receive him. He would not accept his letters. Daniel had reached the end of his admittedly short rope.

He knew very well he had reacted badly to Michael's flippant suggestion that they run away together. It had simply struck him utterly by surprise. The idea of leaving all he had worked so hard for hit hard, made him wonder at his path.

Harder still, though, was the look on Michael's face as he saw it over the barrel of a dueling pistol. Michael had put on a good façade, but it was patently clear he was crushed by Daniel's seemingly casual dismissal of what they had become to each other. Once out, though, Daniel had been unable to think of a convincing way to take it back.

He did condemn himself on occasion for leaving

behind the realm of what was socially acceptable. He did agonize over the knowledge that he would not leave heirs of his own to inherit what he had built from little more than dirt and sweat.

That did not mean he felt unclean for lying with Michael, for loving him.

Throwing himself into his preparations for spring was his only recourse. Finn Hightower had asked him very kindly not to return to the pub until he regained his civility. Samuel Laidlaw abandoned him at the horse auction, telling him to curb his tongue ere they met again. And Jane, well, she had no sympathy for him at all once she heard his sorry tale.

He was in the midst of scrubbing off the worst of the day's grime when he heard the rattle of a carriage outside. His heart leapt, though he forced himself to wait for his servants to announce his visitor. Perhaps Michael had relented.

"Excuse me, sir. Your cousin Jane has arrived."

Daniel sighed, nodding at Calvin. "Very well. Please have her await me downstairs."

"Yes, sir."

Daniel finished his ablutions and assumed his dressing gown over shirtsleeves and trousers, making his way down to the front room. Jane awaited him, tapping her foot impatiently. Her hazel eyes widened upon sight of him.

"You are not dressed. Daniel, do you not recall you promised to accompany me to Squire Madden's ball?"

"Oh, damnation."

"Watch your mouth."

Daniel sighed, crossing his arms and attempting to stare her down. "I have no wish to go."

"But I do." Jane got that obstinate set to her chin, and she stood him down easily. "Go and dress."

"Mule."

"Brainless curmudgeon. You will stop sulking this instant and take me to the ball. I have it on good authority that Michael will be there."

Again his heart set up a rapid beat, and Daniel turned on his heel. "Give me a quarter hour."

It took him little or no time to dress, and he fastened the cravat pin he had yet to return to St. James to his neckcloth. Let the man see how proud he was to be associated with him. How unashamed he was.

Jane surveyed him when he came down, nodding her approval and holding out an imperious hand. He presented his arm, and she took it, sweeping him out.

"You clean up well, cousin."

"I hope you will not be the only one pleased to say so."

She slanted him an amused glance. "Oh, I am sure Madeline Barstow will fawn over you. She has not the sense to leave you be, even when she knows how you dislike her."

"Yes, I know." He scowled. Damn the squawking

hen anyway. "That is not what I meant, though, as you well know."

"I know. But I do remind you to be discreet."

He practically tossed her into the carriage. "Yes, yes. I will. I vow."

"As you say." Jane nudged him with one slippered foot, making him look up and meet her eyes. "I know how you feel, Daniel. Please, please be careful."

She did have his best interests at heart, sympathy or no. Daniel nodded. "For your sake, my dear Jane. I will."

"And for yours."

Daniel made a noise of vague agreement, but for his part he did not care. He had learned what it was to do without Michael St. James now, and he wanted no part of it.

He would rather run away with the man than do without again.

Michael squired some young mouse about the ballroom, promenading with her as she kept her eyes demurely lowered. Damnation, he was bored. He had no idea why he had bothered to attend the blasted ball, except he knew Daniel would be there, and he was so hungry for a look at the man that he was playing the fool.

Whose fault was it that he had not seen Daniel

Calhoun, after all? His own, naturally. He had refused all contact with the man out of sheer stubbornness. What he had come to realize, though, was that he did not care if Daniel was uncertain about them. Michael craved Daniel's presence, and, frankly, he would put up with Daniel's less than stellar opinion of him for the pleasure of it. And because he loved the man beyond care for his own pain.

There. Michael caught a glimpse of mahogany hair and bottle green velvet and turned young Miss Sinclair perhaps too sharply, making her gasp.

"I beg your pardon, sweet. I did not mean to surprise you. I was simply avoiding Mrs. Sharpton, as you requested."

"Oh, thank you." Her cheeks flushed pink, and she smiled at him with perfect coquetry, and all he could think was how she was so very young and not at all his caliber.

"You're quite welcome."

Now he had a fine view of Daniel Calhoun as the man got Jane a glass of punch, and Michael soaked in the sight, taking in the tall strength of his body, the way the green coat and brown breeches outlined it to perfection.

Daniel was frowning at all and sundry. Somehow that made him smile.

He dropped the young miss back with her tittering mother and went to pay his respects to Jane. Sadly, the moment he got close, Daniel disappeared, going to chat with Samuel Laidlaw.

Michael sighed. The avoidance his own fault, again. He had asked Daniel to leave him be.

"Jane, my dear. How are you?"

She looked about quickly before replying, "Better than you, I'll wager. Let us go sit, St. James."

Michael winced. "So I am relegated to last names again, am I?"

"Oh, do be less of an idiot." His arm stung suddenly where she smacked it with her fan, and Michael felt better than he had in days. He followed Jane to a secluded seat and gallantly handed her down.

"I shall try. Do you think he will forgive me if I apologize?"

A most indelicate sound came from her. Michael stared.

"Do not apologize. Tell him you will forgive him if he does. He was intolerable to you, Michael."

Michael stared some more. "I kicked him out at gunpoint."

"Did you really?" Jane gave him a delighted look and a trilling laugh, turning heads in their direction. "How lovely! Good for you! He treated you like a lowly whore, Michael. He deserved as much. I do think, however, Daniel has punished himself far more than you have, and it is time for you to reconcile."

"If you say it, it shall be so." He said it lightly, but Michael agreed wholeheartedly. It was time.

"Then go and find him, Michael. After you

dance with me, of course."

"Of course." Cutting her a bow, he held out an arm. "Shall we?"

"Yes," she said, beaming at him. "We shall."

Formal dancing wore Daniel to the bone. The mincing steps of the slower dances were uniquely unsuited to his large frame, and the vigorous country dances usually saw him flinging his delicate, petticoated partner into orbit about the room like the planets about the sun. Jane told him he was a fine dancer. He chose not to believe her and went outside to hide at every opportunity.

Michael St. James, however, was an excellent dancer. Smooth, supple limbs moved with a skill and coordination Daniel could only envy, and covet. Were he allowed to dance with St. James, he was certain his skill would improve apace. Sadly, he could only watch and envy the ladies who felt the touch of Michael's hand upon their waists, who were able to place their hand in his.

Jealousy surged in his breast, not for the attentions Michael paid them, especially as he had deprived himself of those attentions these last weeks. His jealousy was for those who could be in Michael's shining presence without being forced to hide their admiration, their pleasure in his company. Even if they were to reconcile, he could not look openly on Michael the way he wished.

When Daniel could bear the torture no more, he withdrew, out to the cold gardens, which suited his rough demeanor far more than the glittering ballroom. He watched through the open doors as the colorful creature that was Michael St. James squired a beautiful young lady about the room for a stately promenade, and tried to remember not to grit his teeth. Jane had been bad enough. This child that looked on Michael so adoringly was worse.

The only thing for it was to imagine a dance only he and Michael could do, one that had them nude together in the big bed they had shared up until his faux pas. The thought soothed him even as it excited him. Excited him so his already tight evening trousers became excruciating, pressing against him, digging into his engorged skin, the cold air outside doing nothing to keep him down.

Daniel took a furtive glance about, knowing he should not even consider such a thing, but close association with Michael made him bolder, more reckless, and when no one appeared, Daniel opened the buttons of his trousers, taking out his handkerchief in anticipation of something of a mess.

In his mind he pictured Michael above him, hands and lips and whiskey colored eyes upon him, words falling from those lips as they danced together in their own way. His prick throbbed in his hand at the thought, and Daniel gasped, rubbing, hips moving in time to the movement of his fingers. His hand felt strange, so used to other hands was he, so used to the heat of Michael's mouth, the tight sheath of his body, but if he closed his eyes he could pretend.

Faster and faster he moved, biting his lip to stifle the sound of Michael's name, need tight and heavy in his belly, and when he remembered to open his eyes to keep watch, there was someone there. His heart leapt, beating hard, but it was Michael, his St. James, smiling at him.

He thought at first he was hallucinating, that St. James was a figment of his overheated imagination. But it was not. Indeed, Michael was there, in the flesh, moving to stand with him in the shadows.

"Beautiful, Calhoun. So damned beautiful."

"Michael. I..."

"I know."

Michael moved close, hand coming out to touch him, wrapping about his shaft and pulling. Daniel arched, a soft moan bursting from him as he finally felt Michael's touch after he'd missed it for so long.

Michael dropped to his knees and engulfed him in wet heat, Michael's mouth enclosing him easily, taking him deep. Daniel moaned, and Michael answered him, the vibrations shaking him, tearing at him, and Daniel could hold back no more. He simply bit back a cry and shot, filling Michael's mouth with his seed.

Michael nuzzled him, cheek smooth-shaven

against him, lips soft and swollen. "Come home with me."

"I must...Jane. I must take her home."

"Of course." Michael stood, brushed off his knees, the evidence of his need clearly outlined. "Of course. I am sorry, Daniel, I should not have."

"No!" Grabbing Michael before he could get away, Daniel drew him close, holding him there for a kiss that tasted of his own need and of Michael's desperation. "I am the one who is sorry, Michael. I was wrong."

Michael's eyes glinted in the darkness, searching his face. "I should not have asked."

"And I should not have treated you so. Please. I do need to see Jane home, but I hope you will meet me at mine afterward."

"I will." Michael leaned in, kissed him again, rubbing against his hip. "I will await you most eagerly."

Daniel practically threw Michael down and had him right there. Only a burst of laughter from the house reminded him of where they were, and he did up his buttons, kissing Michael again quickly.

"And I will hurry. I vow it."

They parted with one more kiss, Michael hurrying off and Daniel righting himself, making sure he was presentable so he could go and collect Jane. He had an engagement he did not wish to miss. One that was far more important to him than Jane's desire to mingle with her neighbors.

They were leaving. Now.

Michael waited impatiently in Daniel's front room, refusing the offer of food and drink from Daniel's sleepy servant. He did not need anything but the one thing he did not have yet. Daniel.

He could not believe it had been so simple to come back together. So easy. Perhaps he was mistaken, and it would not be. But as the door opened on a wave of cold air and Daniel was there, enfolding him in that wool and tobacco scent, mouth closing over his, the few weeks of pain and disappointment simply melted away.

Daniel kissed him like there was no other on Earth he had ever wanted. Like there was nothing else on Earth. That was apology enough for him, which was all he could want. When Daniel turned and dragged him up the stairs he did not resist, he simply followed, going up the stairs to Daniel's bedchamber, to Daniel's bed.

They undressed quickly, and Michael though fondly of how his former lovers would laugh to see his fumbling hands now, to hear his panting pleas. He, the always suave one. Not now, not a bit.

Daniel stripped off his shirt, touching his skin, and Michael moaned. "Daniel."

"Yes, St. James?"

"You owe me an apology." Perhaps he needed

to hear it aloud after all.

Nodding, Daniel worked off Michael's trousers and grasped his prick, stroking him lightly. "I do. I am sorry, Michael. I am. I should not have hesitated, not even a moment. You are what I want."

"And you are what I crave."

They struggled with Daniel's clothing, getting him nude as well, falling together on the bed in the manner most popular in the dreadful Italian romances his mother might read. He laughed, and Daniel echoed it, those green eyes glinting.

"How melodramatic we are."

"Yes. I was just thinking that."

Daniel smiled at him, leaning to kiss the corner of his mouth. "I don't care a whit. You, Michael St. James, are a ne'er-do-well, a dandy, and an utter scoundrel. And I find I am quite helplessly taken with you."

"Good. As even though you are a rigid, unbending, country bumpkin, I am utterly without defense against you."

That was most likely as much of a declaration as Michael would ever receive from this man, and he would make do with it. Michael pushed Daniel down, straddling him so he could take kiss after kiss, reveling in the strength under him, at the feel of Daniel's muscles flexing beneath his hands. Daniel's thighs shifted beneath him, and Daniel's thick prick pressed against him, and Michael felt as though he had surely found heaven.

Daniel touched him in return, hands sliding on his skin as they kissed, thumbs on either side of his spine as those hands moved to cup his bottom. He pushed back into the touch, letting Daniel open him, feeling those thick fingers spreading him. They needed oil...perhaps Daniel still had some beside the bed. Michael leaned out for it, found it easily, and looked at Daniel with one brow lifted.

"Self abuse, Calhoun?"

"No. Hoping you would allow me to apologize."

Michael threw back his head and laughed. "Yes. Yes, I will."

Together, they got their fingers oiled, and soon enough Michael had two of Daniel's and one of his own inside him, readying him for Daniel. Daniel's stare was like the sun, heating him to the melting point, and he moved whorishly, the sounds coming from him almost embarrassing in their intensity.

Finally he was prepared and Daniel lifted him up, pushing against him, slipping easily inside him, just as if he was meant to be there. His head fell back, his fingers digging into the skin of Daniel's chest, and they began to move together, neither able to wait a moment more. Daniel pushed up and Michael forced himself down, and Daniel rubbed the spot inside him that simply made him see stars before his eyes.

"Daniel. Please."

"Yes, Michael. Yes."

Daniel's hand closed about his shaft, pulling

in time with their thrusts, and Michael wanted to scream with it, his every nerve alive with need. He rode Daniel hard and fast, trying not to look away, trying to see the expression on Daniel's face, but his eyes blurred with the incredible pleasure. Good Lord, if Daniel ever consented to let Michael take him he might just expire from bliss.

The very thought of sliding into Daniel's untried body was enough to send him over the edge, and Michael cried out sharply, spending in great bursts over Daniel's chest and belly, practically sobbing his pleasure. He felt Daniel's prick moving in him, felt every minute motion as Daniel spent himself as well, hot seed filling him deep. He could only hold himself up with shaking arms and stare down at Daniel, amazed by the force of their passion.

"Daniel, I…"

"No. No more talking for a time, St. James." Daniel pulled him down, held him close, the touch of Daniel's lips on his brow tender, sweet. Utterly unlike any other touch Daniel had ever given him. "We do much better together when we keep the talking to a minimum."

That was true enough, and Michael laughed out loud, curling up along Daniel's side. "We will have to speak on it sometime."

"We will. For now I am content, though."

Yes. Content. Michael was content as well, so he left off, enjoying the feel and smell of them together, and resolving not to ruin their accord by talking too much ever again.

Daniel strode into the pub, feeling better than he had in weeks, a large smile on his face. Whatever their differences, he was glad to have Michael St. James, and he did not care if all who saw him could read it on his face. He was in such a fine mood, in fact, he hardly noticed how few of his acquaintances greeted him with any enthusiasm. It was not unusual, and his mood of late had left many people licking their wounds after running afoul of his ill temper.

'Twas not until Finn refused to serve him that he realized aught was amiss.

"Your money is no good here, Calhoun," Finn said, spitting noisily at the spittoon. "I'd just as soon you'd leave."

He stared. He had known Finn all of his life, had delivered two calves and a goat kid for the man just last spring. There had never been any trouble between them.

"What are you talking about? Draw me a pint, man."

Finn just turned his back, and when Daniel looked about to see what the other inhabitants of the pub might say, no one would look him in the eye.

Not one of them.

A chill ran up his spine, but Daniel refused to give into the blank stares and averted eyes, turning back to Finn.

"What is this about, Finn?"

"You ought to know, and if you don't you're worse than I thought. Now kindly leave."

He wanted to protest that he had no idea what Finn was talking about, but he had a feeling he did know, and it made him furious. His hands clenched into fists.

"Very well, Finn. But I will thank you to remember a few things after I go. Perhaps think about who kept your milk cow from dying, or about who set your son's leg when he fell in the creek and broke it."

Let the man think on that for a bit, and see if it did not make him feel like a hypocrite. Daniel turned on his heel, fairly shaking with rage, and left, his head held high. He would not let these people make him feel guilty for loving Michael St. James. Daniel stopped just outside the door, shock holding him immobile.

Love.

Good gad.

Yet that was what it was. He loved Michael beyond all reason.

Damnation. He needed to warn the man about the change of tenor in town. Right away, if the black looks he'd gotten were any indication. He could handle anything they threw at him, but he would not have Michael injured through any fault of his. Not at all.

He mounted his horse and spurred him toward Michael's home. It looked as though they were going to have to discuss things. He only hoped it ended better than their last talk.

Michael stopped by the parish church to pay his respects to the good pastor and to apologize for not attending of late. He'd been avoiding Calhoun, after all, and he admitted he had taken it rather too far. It was time for him to rejoin society, such as it was, and church was a good place to start.

"Good afternoon, sir," he called to Pastor Lawrence as the man came around the corner from the priory.

The good pastor started, looking at him wide-eyed. "Mister St. James," the man stammered. "What do you want?"

That was an odd enough greeting that Michael looked at the man askance. "I was just stopping by to apologize for my absence."

"Oh." Lawrence shrugged. "Perhaps it is best you do not attend, if you have no desire to repent."

"No desire to…" Michael tilted his head, regarding the man as if he were a zoo animal. Really, people were an odd bunch. "I am not certain I understand."

The man shifted from one foot to another, wringing his hands, before finally looking as though he had made a decision, nodding slightly. Lawrence came forward and put a hand out to him, looking as earnest as only a man of the cloth could.

"You must give up your evil ways, St. James. Come, we will pray on it together."

He stared at that pink hand for long moments before very deliberately crossing his arms. "Which evil ways would those be, good sir? Those in which I cook and eat children, or the ones that cause me to turn into a wolf on the full moon?"

"This is not an amusing matter, St. James."

"Really?" Michael sighed. "And just what is the matter, sir?"

"You. Your behavior. With…that man."

His heart sank. Obviously in their recent exuberance at being together once more, he and Daniel had been less than discreet.

"I see. Well, my behavior is none of your business, Pastor Lawrence."

"You do not even deny it! You could be jailed for this sir. But worse than that, your immortal soul is in danger. You mustn't carry this any farther."

Michael drew himself up. "Thank you for your concern, sir, but it is unnecessary. My loyalty lies elsewhere, you see. Good day to you."

He left the good man stewing, mounting up again and heading for Daniel's home. It looked as though they had a great deal to discuss.

Damnation, he hated it when people took it upon themselves to be judge and jury. Who were he and Daniel hurting? No one. They were both fully capable of making their own decisions. It was not as if he had seduced a green boy, and there was no one to challenge him on Daniel's behalf, no one to injure and be run out of town, disowned yet again.

Michael cursed steadily all the long ride out to Daniel's farm, cursed again when the serving boy told him Daniel was away from home. He scribbled a note quickly and left. He would await Daniel in the comfort of his own home, where he knew the servants well enough to know they would not speak on his situation.

The ride home seemed endless, but it was all made worthwhile when he saw Daniel exiting his front door, riding crop slapping against his boot.

"There you are, St. James. I fear we must talk."

"You too, hmm?"

Daniel looked at him, head tilted. "Did someone give you trouble as well."

"Yes. May we go in and talk on it over brandy?" He dismounted and tossed the reins to his groom. "I feel the need to have a toddy."

"Of course." They walked back inside together, and once in, Daniel turned and took his arms, pulling him up for a kiss that nearly sent him senseless.

"What was that for?" he asked, breathless and flushed.

"To remind you of what is important before we talk and cock things up again."

Delighted, he took Daniel's gloved hand in his and led him into the study, hollering for Elias on the way. Once Elias was dispatched to fetch them hot drinks, they sat, both of them pulling off coats and gloves before settling.

"Well," Daniel began. "I was thoroughly snubbed at the Fox and Hound this afternoon."

"Were you?" Damn. Damn and damn. Michael tried to maintain a calm façade, but he was quite worried, if truth be told. "Pastor Lawrence threatened me with eternal damnation."

Daniel stared for a moment, then burst out laughing, the deep, raucous sound so infectious he found himself smiling along. Daniel slapped his knee and laughed until he had tears streaming down his face.

"Oh, dear. I must say that being denied a pint and being tossed into the lake of eternal fire are two very different things, St. James. How glad I am that I am not you."

"Yes, yes, laugh while you can. I am sure were you to darken the good holy man's door you would hear the same sermon."

"Oh, I don't doubt it." Daniel sobered. "I would not see you injured or harmed due to this, Michael, and people are just ignorant enough to try."

"I thought the same of you."

Again they stared at one another, in accord

about their concerns, which was rather amusing in its own right. Daniel seemed more worried about him than about what people thought, which told Michael that Daniel's professed change of attitude about being with him was very real indeed.

He found the change terrifying.

"So, what shall we do?" Daniel sat forward, elbows on his knees. "I will not give you up, so do not even suggest it."

"No, that was not what I was going to suggest. What I was thinking of, however, was a very public falling out. If people saw us disassociate from one another, then we might be able to control the damage to your reputation."

It would mean sneaking about afterward, and never, ever being seen in public again together, but it would indeed repair what had been broken, he was sure. People would continue to treat him as a pariah, but that he was accustomed to, where Daniel was not.

"Absolutely not. If you think I will let these people force me to live more of a lie than we do you are sadly mistaken, St. James."

Daniel often told him Jane had an obstinate chin. That dear lady had nothing on Daniel Calhoun. Michael sighed and sipped the drink Elias handed him, feeling the brandy burn all the way to his gut. The sugar in it tempered the fire not at all.

"Well, then, we are at an impasse, because I refuse to be the cause of you losing everything you hold dear."

"I hold Jane dear. I hold my new cousin, little Henry, dear. My land. And you. So if you force me into some farce where we cannot even go to auction together, you will be the cause of it. There is nothing they can take away from me that I will more willingly give than their company, believe me."

That was true enough. "But what about feed, tack, supplies?"

"I can go to Richmond. The rumors will not follow me there."

"But…"

"No." Daniel cut him off firmly, tossing back his toddy before coming to pull him out of his seat, so close he could see each individual whisker on Daniel's cheek, each stubby black eyelash. "Just no, St. James. I intend to have you whenever I want. Not when society dictates."

How could he argue with the intent in Daniel's eyes, with the certainty in his voice? He could not, and so he did not. He simply put his hand to Daniel's cheek and nodded.

"Very well, then. We weather the storm."

Daniel kissed him by way of agreement, pulling him up so his toes nearly left the floor. When the kiss ended he stood so close they could not tell where one ended and the other began, his hands buried in Daniel's walnut hair, one of Daniel's thighs pressed between his.

Daniel searched his face, and whatever he saw

satisfied him, for he got a nod and another kiss, this one sweet and deep and long.

"Yes, St. James," Daniel said. "Weather it we will."

Despite his certainty that nothing could cause him damage he could not withstand, Daniel was determined to find out who was behind the sudden knowledge the community seemed to have of his affairs. So he went to the closest thing he had to a finger on the pulse of said community. Samuel Laidlaw.

"I am sorry, Sir. He is from home."

Daniel scowled at the servant, who looked somewhat cowed. Damnation.

"I know he is here, as I saw him in the yard when I came about. Tell that miserable whoreson if he does not see me, I will file his gambling debts to me with the debtor's prison."

"Now, now, Daniel. There is no need for that." Samuel's gruff voice came from within. "Let him in, blast you."

The servant stepped aside, twitching nervously as he strode inside. Samuel was standing in the hall, post in hand, glaring at him powerfully. Daniel refused to be cowed by his old friend.

"So, who in bloody blazes is talking, Samuel?"

"Who is not?"

Samuel motioned him into the study, closing the door firmly behind them. "Damn it, Daniel. How could you be so stupid? At the Squire's ball no less?"

His cheeks heated. Well, that explained a great deal. Someone had seen them, then. "Yes, I suppose that was ill-advised. Still, most people would not spread it far and wide this quickly. It smacks of maliciousness."

"Of course it does." Collapsing into a chair, Samuel put his bad leg up on the tufted stool he kept for just that purpose. "I do not know how you intend to salvage this, Daniel, but I vow you will have trouble like you have not had ere now. Perhaps he could leave town?"

"No. I think not. What I do is my business."

Damnation, he hated this. Why did people insist upon sticking their nose in?

"Not when most see it was illegal and immoral."

"And you, Samuel? Do you see me as a changed man? Someone to be shunned and feared? Are you afraid I shall taint you?"

"Do not be any more ridiculous than you must be, Daniel." Samuel waved to a chair. "'My servant did not want to let you in. What I do not see is an easy way for you to get out of this if you continue to be with him."

"I will not give him up."

"Then be prepared to suffer the consequences."

Daniel looked Samuel right in the eye and nodded. "So be it."

Michael went to Madeline Barstow's home, determined to talk to the bitch about his misfortune, for he felt sure he could lay it firmly at her door. It was one thing for her jealousy to fall upon him, but quite another for it to complicate Daniel's life.

She met him in her boudoir, wearing a diaphanous dress gown that left nothing to the imagination. Michael wanted to gag. She held her bony arms out to him, and he fended her off, watching her pout as she flounced into a chair.

"I was hoping you'd come to see me, Michael."

"Really? Why is that, Madeline?"

"Don't be coy, Michael."

He looked at her pouty, painted mouth, and her shorn hair, growing out in Medusa-like coils as she went from wearing wigs to wearing her hair in the new Empress style. She made him cringe.

"Very well, Madeline. I shall be blunt. I know you are the one who has set out to ruin us. What I do not understand is why. Is it because he spurned you? Is it because I stopped squiring you about to soirees? Or are you simply bored?"

She studied her nails, a small smile playing about her mouth. "I do it because it amuses me. I believe you shocked even me, Michael, when I saw you on your knees at the Squire's ball."

"It amuses you to ruin a man's life."

He could not help the tone, at once incredulous and disdainful.

"Why, Michael, you are quite ruined already." She smiled, the look unpleasant in the extreme. "And Calhoun has often said in my hearing that he cares not a whit what others think of him."

"This is his home, Madeline. You and I are but passing through, and you know it. What will he do when we leave and his reputation is irreparable?"

Madeline leaned forward, showing off her bony chest and shrunken cleavage in an obvious attempt to be seductive. Michael shuddered, and her eyes narrowed.

"You see, the difference between you and I, Michael, is that you care." She stabbed a finger at him. "You used to be such *fun*."

"You amaze me." Michael rose, drawing his coat and his dignity around him. "I advise you to reconsider your gossip-mongering ways, Madeline. At the risk of sounding like my dear sainted father, what goes around comes around. Your love of others' misery will someday result in your own. I know from experience."

She rose as well, going to stand next to the door in an obvious dismissal. "Get out. Do not count upon me to retract my statements, either. I rather like the way this is turning out."

"Yes. I imagine you do."

He swept out, head held high. Threatening her would do no good, though his hands itched to wrap around her neck and squeeze the breath out so she could no longer speak filth about him. About Daniel.

He would simply have to find some way of discrediting her, and the dozens of other people who had spread her no doubt lurid stories.

There had to be a way.

"I am sorry, Mister Daniel. Missus Jane is not receiving."

"I beg your pardon?" Daniel stared at the maid, Lucy, who opened the door at Jane and Gerard's home. "Is she ill?"

"Not that I know, Sir. I was just told by Mister Gerard that she wasn't seeing anyone."

"Well, then, show me in and tell Mister Gerard that I am here."

The girl looked behind her nervously before stepping aside to let him in. All in all it was most strange behavior. Perhaps it was Lucy who was ill. Daniel handed her his hat and gloves. "I will await him in the drawing room."

He went to the drawing room and paced, worried that Jane was ill, or perhaps Henry. It was not like Jane not to see him, at least, and while it was not unusual for Gerard to forbid her visitors, usually the man would at least explain why himself.

Gerard left him cooling his heels long enough that he was ready to start bellowing for Jane just as the man appeared. Daniel started to greet him warmly, only to trail off when Gerard would not meet his eyes, standing far away and shifting foot to foot instead.

"Oh, for Heaven's sake, Gerard. Not you too!"

Gerard was family. Surely he would not do this.

"Oh, Daniel." Gerard looked at him, a miserable expression in his washed out eyes. "I am sorry. It's only that I must think of Henry now, mustn't I? You know Jane and my position here is tenuous at best. And what they accuse you of..."

"What is that, Gerard? They accuse me of loving someone entirely inappropriate? I believe you heard the exact same complaints when you married so far beneath you with Jane."

"That is not at all the same, and you know it. I must protect my family."

"Are you saying," Daniel moved closer, towering over Gerard's slight form, "that you think I would harm Jane or little Henry?"

"Of course he is not. He is simply being an ass."

Daniel turned, relief flooding him. "Jane."

She came right to him and put a hand on his arm, giving Gerard a look that would scorch any man it fell upon. "I know you would never hurt any of us. How are you? It must be awful." Jane embraced him.

"I am most annoyed."

She had the temerity to giggle at him. "Only you could have people discussing your life and accusing you of such odious things well beyond what you are doing and be annoyed."

"Well, what would you have of me? I am not ashamed."

"I do not want you to be. Most people, however, would be devastated. You never cease to amaze me."

Giving the sputtering Gerard another look, Jane linked arms with him. "Walk with me."

He strolled off with her, down the hall to her dainty morning room, where he felt entirely out of place. Gerard felt just as uncomfortable there, though, and so would not follow.

"You must deal with this, Daniel. The whole of the parish is talking about you, and I fear your reputation was such that it cannot withstand the blow."

He stared. "You are blaming this on me?"

"Damnation, Daniel! He was...you were together, intimately, outside the ball! Do you deny it?"

"No." That had been stupid in the extreme, he could not deny it, but he would not apologize for it. "So what do you suggest? Am I to stay away from you as well?"

"Of course not, though I must admit that Gerard is appalled, more at your lack of discretion than at your activities. But you mustn't be seen with him."

"You and Samuel Laidlaw. I will not live my life in hiding."

She turned on him, hands on her hips. "Then you will not live it here. These people will not tolerate it. You could be imprisoned for it should they decide you pushed it too far."

"Jane." He ran a hand through his hair, a goodly bit of it coming loose from the club at the back of his neck. He still could not seem to fall in with the newly shorn fashion. Michael said he was stubbornly Saxon when the rest of the world was going Norman. "I do not know what you want from me."

"I want you to understand the consequences of this, Daniel. It could be the end of you here."

He simply stared at her. Out of all of the people he expected to condemn him, she was not one. Yet that was what it felt like.

"I see. Am I allowed to darken your door in the future?"

"Do not be more of an imbecile than you must." She had the brass to hit him. It rather stung. "Of course you can. But, Daniel, you must."

"I know," he interrupted. "I know. Tell Gerard not to try to lock me out."

Without another word, Daniel turned on his heel and left, feeling wounded. Jane was always his staunchest supporter. Having her rail against him, even as she defied Gerard, was lowering. He had always counted on her unwavering support. And now she had wavered.

He went straight home, knowing Michael would be waiting for him. They had agreed to meet there for supper. He spurred his horse on, needing Michael's presence, knowing it would be a balm to his spirit. Together they would work something out that did not include hiding. He was sure of it.

Michael paced, awaiting Daniel, his meeting with Madeline Barstow eating away at him. The bitch. What else could he call her? Obviously she had set her sights upon making them miserable, because she herself was a miserable, dried up old woman. The problem was that even as odious as she was, she was more socially acceptable than he ever would be, and he was uncertain as to how they might fight her influence.

He feared he would wear a hole in the braided rug in the front room before Daniel came home. Studying the handmade furniture and simple, clean ornaments in the room only depressed his spirits more. The room reflected Daniel so perfectly it reinforced how Daniel belonged here. And how he himself did not.

The door opened on Daniel, who scowled fearsomely until he saw Michael. The smile that broke through then did a great deal to brighten his own dark mood. Michael went to him to take a kiss.

"Well, you look as though your mission was as unsuccessful as mine," Michael said, putting his arms about Daniel's neck.

"It was edifying to be sure."

Edifying. Oh, dear. "How so?"

"Gerard did not want to let me in. Even Jane berated me." Daniel's eyes went dark. "Jane, Michael. I could not fathom it."

How well he remembered that feeling. His father's wrath he could bear. His mother's quiet disappointment had cut him to the bone. The sting of Jane's disapproval and Gerard's betrayal would stay with Daniel for some time. Michael could not help but feel it was his fault. "I am sorry, Daniel."

"So am I, Michael. Sorry that people are ignorant fools."

He smiled wryly, stroking Daniel's cheek. "Oh, come, Daniel. If it were not you, and you heard about such things as we do, what would you think?"

"What an entirely unfair question."

That scowl was so like the ones he had gotten when they first met, and Michael could not help but smile. "Why is it unfair?"

"Because it is me, and it is Jane, and she has ever been my champion. I would not turn against her, even if she told me she was leaving Gerard and going off to join a Shaker colony."

That made him laugh aloud. "Oh, Daniel, you

would rant and rave."

"I would. But in the end I would support her decision, and I would never turn her away from my home. Never."

"No, you would not, would you?" He stroked Daniel's cheek once more, fingers tracing every line and whisker. "My fiercely loyal Calhoun."

"Bah." Bending to kiss him, Daniel pulled him close, rubbing against him most suggestively. "Let's forget this for a time, hmm? We shall decide what to do later."

Kissing Daniel right back, Michael nodded, letting Daniel lead him upstairs. He knew exactly what he would do. And it quite broke his heart.

Daniel took Michael by the hand and took him up to his rooms, fearing the look on his face. Somehow he had the idea Michael was about to do something very stupid indeed, and he wanted to take his mind off it completely.

He wanted to take his own mind off things as well. They would find a way to get through all of this cock and bull nonsense, Daniel knew they would, but right now, at this moment, it all seemed too much.

They gained his bedchamber and Michael turned to him without a word, one hand coming up to cup his cheek. They kissed, their mouths opening for one another, tongues touching and sliding, and it was the most natural thing. Daniel found it impossible to believe he had once found it unnatural. He clutched Michael to him. No one would take this from him. No one.

Michael did not protest his too enthusiastic hold. No, indeed. In fact, St. James clung just as hard, bruising Daniel's lips with the force of his kiss. By the end of it, they were both gasping, trying to catch their breath and staring at one another wordlessly.

Something flashed in Michael's eyes, something that turned them from clear amber to dark fire, and Michael tore at his neckcloth before grabbing the front of his shirt and yanking, sending studs flying in all directions. His gaze followed one of the onyx pieces as it bounced, and while his attention was elsewhere, Michael shoved him, sending him reeling back toward the bed.

His back hit the mattresses, and his breath left him. Daniel leaned, watching as Michael stripped down, pale skin appearing under waistcoat and shirt, trousers and smallclothes falling to the floor. Like milk. Wasn't that what the poets said? Michael's skin was like milk. But there the comparison to womanly charms stopped. His chest was wide, his shoulders broad, though not so broad as Daniel's own, and his narrow waist and long legs fairly made Daniel drool.

There was no more time to look, though, as

St. James advanced upon him, pushing him until he hoisted himself up on the bed so that Michael could yank off his boots and trous. Michael bent, rough cheek rubbing against his prick, and Daniel gasped, his whole body singing. His back arched, his toes curled, and Michael laughed.

St. James was ever aware of his own power.

Climbing up on the bed with him, Michael stroked his belly, staring at him for a moment.

"I would have you, Daniel."

"You always do."

"No. I mean I would take you. I want to be inside you."

His heart stuttered in his chest. He had never given that. Michael had never asked it before. In his mind he could see all of the times they had been together, Michael above him or beneath him, taking him in, hot and deep and better than anything...

Reaching up, he stroked Michael's cheek, as tender a touch as he had ever given. "Yes."

Michael's breath came in sharply and he turned, kissing Daniel's hand. His palm tingled where Michael's lips pressed, and Daniel shivered. The look on Michael's face...

It burned him.

"You will not regret it, Daniel, I vow."

"How could I?"

Michael bent, lips pressing against his in a kiss that tightened every muscle in his body. Michael touched him everywhere, fingers soft on his throat and shoulders, harder as they pressed the flat nipples on his chest. Where the hands led, Michael's mouth followed, tasting him everywhere, lips and tongue and teeth moving over him. His nipples ached and throbbed, and tiny bruises rose under Michael's touch, marring his chest and belly.

When Michael touched his prick Daniel moaned, the sound loud, desperate, and shocking to him in light of St. James' utter silence. He could barely hear Michael breathing. Michael's hand closed about him, stroking, squeezing, making him rise up on his heels and on the back of his neck and shoulders, trying to get more of the sensation. Then Michael's mouth was on him, and he was crying out, shaking as he tried to hold back until Michael finished with him, trying not to spend himself too soon.

Wicked. The only possible word for Michael St. James' mouth was wicked. It worked on him, devoured him, did things no proper mouth should do. His balls rolled off the flat of Michael's tongue and Daniel heard himself whimper. Really. What a very ridiculous sound to have come from his own throat.

Finally, Michael moved beyond all bounds of decency, mouth slipping beneath his sac to touch him so intimately that the sounds coming from him changed to shock.

"Michael! St. James. Stop."

Looking up at him, Michael licked his lips. "Why? I must prepare you, Daniel. I wish to taste you. Will you deny me this?"

Those eyes. How they pleaded with him, no trace of the usual deviltry in them. Only need. Daniel shook.

"No. No, do as you will, St. James."

Michael simply smiled, nodded, bending to him again, and Daniel stroked Michael's hair as his body gave over to the unspeakable pleasure Michael visited on him.

He had no idea how long it went on, but Michael rose above him finally, pressing his thighs so wide the muscles protested. Daniel let himself be spread, looking up at Michael as St. James settled against him. Michael stared down at him, lips rosy, cheeks flushed.

"I will not hurt you, Daniel. Never that."

"I know." He knew that, with a deep certainty. Just as he knew that if he did this something would change irrevocably within him. Still, he forged ahead. "Please."

"Yes."

The broad head of Michael's prick pierced him, opened him unbearably. Daniel thought of how easily Michael took him and concentrated on relaxing himself so Michael might slide right in. Breathing deeply, he bore down, and finally he heard a sound from Michael, a long, indrawn breath as Michael pushed home, seating deep within him.

Daniel arched, muscles bunching, trying to ease the ache deep inside. Then Michael began to move and the ache became so much greater, so much deeper, until he could hardly bear it. A tearing noise escaped him, and Michael bent to kiss him, the feel and taste of Michael on his tongue helping to distract him.

The sensations overwhelmed him, made him sweat and pant. The deep thrusts Michael made into his body became gradually more a pleasure than a pain, and when Michael's hand wrapped about his own prick and pulled, Daniel knew he had found heaven.

No wonder such things were discouraged. Nothing that felt like this should be allowed on mere Earth.

Michael gasped out his name, hand clenching upon him, and Daniel's eyes rolled in his head as he spent across Michael's palm, his body shuddering and shaking. He could feel Michael, deep within him, wet and hot, each pulse of Michael's prick ringing through him.

He heard Michael sob. Then St. James went limp, collapsing down on his chest. Daniel caught him instinctively, so exhausted that his arms shook.

"St. James." His voice shook as well. "Michael."

Michael looked up from where he lay on Daniel's chest, blinking slowly, eyes dazed. "Yes, Daniel Calhoun. I know."

Michael eased away from Daniel once he knew Daniel slept deep, grabbing up his clothes and sneaking into the dressing room to assume all but his shoes. Then he crept out like a thief, making sure even the stairs did not creak under his feet.

He needed a good start, for he had no doubt the stubborn fool man that was Daniel Calhoun would try to find him. At least to begin with. He was almost out the front door when it occurred to him that he should write whatever missive he would leave for Daniel while he was here.

The letter was a matter of moments in the writing, and he found no end of irony in sealing the silly thing with the seal he had gifted Daniel with at Christmas.

It was not until he was on his mount and on his way to his rented home to pack his meager belongings that Michael allowed himself a sour laugh, making his horse sidestep.

Michael St. James, doing the noble thing.

What, he wondered, would his sainted father think of that?

Chapter Nine

The fire did little to warm him, and Daniel pulled his coat tighter about his body. The inn he stayed at tonight was barely adequate, and Daniel chose to sleep before the fire in the commons room rather than share a tiny chamber with four or five smelly strangers, cheap as the rooms may be. He had no anticipation of trouble from the few rabble-rousers still about. His appearance was such these last weeks that he intimidated even the footpads. Unshaven, creased and wrinkled, and constantly scowling, lacking sleep, surly, Daniel knew he looked as bad if not worse than the worst element he should find in a place such as this.

Tossing back a glass of brandy was safer than savoring it, bad as it was, and that was exactly what he did. With stiff, cold fingers he drew out Michael's letter and read it once again, still overcome with disbelief at its contents. Damn the man straight to Hell. The ink was almost gone in places, rubbed away by Daniel's fingers, as if by touching the words he could come to understand why the thrice-damned idiot had left him. Not that it ever worked, certainly. Touching even so small a part of Michael gave him hope, however minute, that he might see the man again. Even if it was just to strangle him.

It was not as if he needed to be able to see the words to read them. He had committed them to memory.

"My Dearest Daniel," it read:

I know you will not understand this. Will, in fact, rage about it, and quite possibly scare your servants half unto death. It is, however, something I must do. Without making a dramatic scene for the benefit of your neighbors, I am leaving. After that vicious harpy, Madeline Barstow, and I talked, and I could not sway her from telling all and sundry how she saw us, I realized I have put you in jeopardy of losing your credibility and reputation in your community, which would hurt you greatly. I have no desire to do that. If I am gone, the scandal, such as it is now, will blow over quickly and will be forgotten in a matter of weeks. Please understand if I stayed it would become increasingly difficult to hide what we had, and such risks cannot be borne. You may think so, of course, but I do not. For all of your protests, you love your land, and were I the cause of you losing it you would come to hate me. This I could not bear.

I took the liberty of taking some funds out of your desk. I have little ready cash, and at this time of the night I doubt I shall find any. I have left you my pearls, in exchange for the money. My mother did give them to me to sell, after all, and if they serve to remind you of me, all the better. You may go to the home I have been renting and collect them from Elias. By the by, if you have a position for him, he is a good man and will serve you well. I can no longer afford to pay him, and I will leave him with the month's rental paid on the house so he may close it for me.

I pray you will understand and forgive. I am deeply sorry to have caused this mess. The least I can do is set it to rights.

Yours in all things,

Michael

One thing he certainly did understand. Michael St. James was a melodramatic, selfish imbecile. Sneaking out in the middle of the night on the basis of a few rumors, spread by a relative newcomer to the county, and one not well liked in the main. True, people had been less than accommodating, but running away only gave people reason to believe their self-righteous judgment was correct.

Which was, no doubt, why he had run away himself, chasing the man down. Delaware, of all places. Delaware was miserable. Cold and wet and, frankly, a shit hole. Even when spring was taking hold down in Virginia, Delaware remained horrid.

He tucked the note back into the thick packet holding his papers and Michael's pearls and held his hands out to the fire to warm them. Shit hole or no, it was where he would find Michael. If the man stayed true to the pattern he had established in his travels, Daniel would catch up to him tomorrow in Wilmington. Tonight he would try to sleep and perhaps have pleasant dreams for the first time in well over a fortnight.

Dreams of strangling Michael St. James to death, which he no doubt deserved, or killing him with a good, hard mattress pounding, which was what Daniel truly wished to do.

The morning dawned long before Daniel was prepared to wake, but wake he did, and he browbeat the innkeeper into a hot meal and hotter basin of water. Caring for his horse and paying his bill took less than half an hour, and he was soon on the road again, turning his face toward Wilmington and the fine hotel Michael was no doubt ensconced in. Damn the man to Hell and back, it was freezing and blustery and Daniel cursed himself for eight kinds of a fool for not just letting the man go. Such was love, he supposed, and sourly at that.

The weather was foul, and Daniel would have sold what was left of his soul to see a ribbon of sunshine. By the time he reached Wilmington, he was wet, cold through, and very, very out of sorts.

A few inquiries led him to a moderately priced inn, and Daniel laughed, watching his breath crystallize before his face. Michael must be running out of money. He could not manage it to save him.

Small favors, Daniel supposed, because it was that very thing which slowed Michael down enough for Daniel to catch him up. Michael had sold his stallion after the first few days on the road and had bought a cheaper mount, which made him much slower and made his stops along the way longer, for his horse needed a day to recover between trips. Daniel had found the stallion his fourth day on the road, bought him back from the squire who'd purchased him, and was boarding him there until he and Michael came back through.

The room was the best in the house, naturally. At the end of the hall on the upper floor, for which Daniel was grateful. Less chance of some passerby hearing the sound of Michael choking as Daniel strangled him. Yes, it would do nicely. He knocked, more softly than was his wont, hoping it would sound like a timid innskeep.

His first reaction upon seeing Michael whole was relief. Concern followed closely upon relief's heels, because the man was pale and thin and looked like he might collapse at the sight of Daniel Calhoun on his doorstep. The feeling he finally settled upon was righteous anger. They stood there, staring, and Daniel finally decided Michael would not do the decent thing and speak first.

"Unless you want that scene you ran off to avoid, St. James, I suggest you let me in."

Wordlessly, Michael stepped back and let him through the door, watching Daniel as if he could not quite believe his eyes. Once inside, Daniel peeled off the sodden weight of his coat and went to warm his hands at the small stove. After several tense minutes wherein Michael stood still and silent as a wax effigy, Daniel finally spoke again.

"You led me a merry chase, I must say."

"You weren't supposed to chase me, you know." Michael's voice was raw, pained.

"Yes, I did get that impression." Silence reigned again for long moments. Then Daniel exploded. "You damned fool idiot! How dare you? How dare you do this and say that it was for my own good? If you wanted to leave me, then all good and well. Goodbye to you and Godspeed. But by damn, sir, you should have the strength of character to tell me instead of sneaking away like a dog in the night. If instead, as I suspect, you are doing this out of some misguided sense of loyalty to me, you picked a fine bloody time to grow a noble soul. I liked you better as a rakehell."

Spots of bright color appeared on Michael's cheeks during the tirade, and when Daniel was done, he blasted right back, which made something deep inside Daniel loosen. If they were arguing, he and St. James, there was hope.

"Whatever evidence you may have to the contrary, Calhoun, I can be a decent man. I left for the sake of your reputation. You have family there. A home. Standing. I could not bear to cause you the pain of losing it like I... Well, suffice to say I knew it would be better if I left."

"Horsefeathers." Daniel forced his smile away as Michael turned an incredulous look upon him. "You ran out of fear. Not so much for me, but for you. You feared I would choose them over you, just as your father did, so you left before I knew there was a choice to be made."

"Will you not accord me a single shred of decency? I can be honorable, you know."

Belligerent still, but now hurt. Bullheaded, stubborn, blind fool. "I know that, Michael. I merely propose that in this case your honor was misguided by fear."

"You are by far the most annoying man I have ever met."

"Then we are well matched."

Silence fell again, lengthening while each one plotted their next move. Michael still stood a goodly distance away, arms crossed, stance rigidly erect. Time for a flanking maneuver.

"I love you a great deal, you know," Daniel began, ignoring Michael's gasp. "I have for some time now." He advanced, so slowly as to be unnoticeable, or at least Michael was too distracted to remark on it. "When you left, I first thought you were bored and so decided to leave me, hoping I would feel you had done it for good reasons. Propriety not being your strong suit, it took me some time to realize you were doing it for exactly the reason you said you were. That is when I realized how frightened you must be of that very community you were leaving me to. At that moment I decided to hunt you down and find you and force my presence upon you until you took me with you."

When he finished, Daniel was positioned precisely where he wished, directly in front of Michael, close enough to breathe the same air. It was air flavored with Michael's growing panic.

"But you love it there."

"No, I loved having my own place. My own piece of land. There is nothing that says I cannot have that elsewhere. Have we not had this conversation before? No matter. We will have it until you believe me."

Reaching out, Michael very nearly touched him, eyes flaring with hope in that single moment. Then he frowned and drew back. "Wait. You say that as if it is in the past. Why?"

"I deeded the land to Jane before I left."

"You what?" Whiskey eyes alight with a fine rage, Michael poked him in the chest. "Of all the stupid, idiotic... Oh, damn you, Daniel Calhoun. You can never leave well enough alone. Do you think I shall thank you for this grand gesture? Do you think I could live with you, knowing that every day you would come to resent me for taking away all you hold dear? I will not have it."

"The grand gesture, you utter fool, should tell you that you are what I hold most dear. I think I shall have to kiss you now."

Michael fought him at first, but not hard enough to be convincing, opening to the kiss after only a cursory struggle. A low, needy sound escaped Daniel as he pulled Michael close, wrapping an arm around his waist, using his other hand to tilt Michael's head for the best angle to deepen the kiss, to push his lover's mouth open and take everything he had missed and wanted and dreamed of for a long, miserable time.

Michael simply melted against him, clinging, kissing with equal fervor, and Daniel felt a desperate need to see and touch that soft, white skin, to assure himself this was indeed his Michael, that the whole scenario was not a figment of his fevered imagination.

He broke away from the kiss, struggling out of his own sodden garments, practically ripping Michael's from his body. There was no furious protest about the fine cloth being damaged, no sardonic remark, simply clumsy hands tangled with his and soft, hot words breathed across his skin.

His own violent need birthed an answering necessity in Michael, and they fell together on the creaky inn bed, kissing furiously, touching frantically, practically mindless in their attempt to familiarize themselves once more with the scent and feel and taste of one another. Michael was thinner, his ribs more prominent, his belly concave, but he smelled the same, and his skin was, as ever, soft as that of a fine lady indulging in daily milk baths.

The taste was what he had missed the most, however. The salt and musk, with a hint of strong soap and bay rum. Michael was less than clean-shaven himself, and the rough bristles on his face caught at Daniel's skin. His nipples were hard, his skin flushing a dark red, and his cock...oh, that glorious cock, quivering for him. He had to taste that as well, and he did, curling around Michael's needy body, putting his mouth on the man, making him shout.

The flavor was stronger there, hotter, as addictive as opium. Michael's hands on him felt good and right, and he arched into the touch of Michael's fingers on his own needy shaft as Michael turned neatly, aligning them head to hip. Soft, hot lips slid along the head of his cock, driving him utterly mad with lust, making him keen around the flesh in his mouth, closing a circle of pleasure that left them both gasping.

Soon, too soon, it was over, his climax crashing through him with staggering intensity, pouring out of him into Michael, even as Michael released into his greedy mouth. It left him stunned, unable to think, barely able to breathe. Turning, he brought Michael up alongside him, engulfing him in a tight embrace, and for the first time in nearly a month's time, he slept quickly and deeply. He did not dream.

The clack of the door latch lifting woke Daniel in the hour just before dawn, and thank goodness it did. "May I inquire," he asked loudly, "where you are going at this time of the day? Especially carrying your boots instead of wearing them? I imagine that makes for cold feet."

Sighing, Michael closed the door. "I was leaving you, naturally."

"Again. For my own good." Damn the man for doing everything in the wee hours of the bloody morning. Daniel struggled to think. There had to be something. Ah. Yes. He smiled. That would work.

"Quite." Michael's countenance nearly broke his heart. Dejection was writ large there, as well as in the sagging line of his shoulders. Daniel could not afford to weaken now, despite the pitiful nature of Michael's look. It was time to play his very last stratagem, in hopes that it would checkmate the king.

"I see." Daniel sat up, feeling the cold of the room prickle at his skin. "Stir the fire up, would you?"

St. James did, moving like an automaton. Nerves settled heavily in Daniel's stomach, sitting there like any number of the gut-turning meals he had eaten on the road of late, but he steeled himself for what he was about to do. It simply must work. Once Michael seated himself in the hard ladderback chair across the room, Daniel began.

"So. Not only have you besmirched my good name in my home, you have stolen from me, lied to me, sullied what was left of my dubious virtue, and to add insult to certain injury, you were going to sneak off and leave me to pay the bill at this fleabitten excuse for an inn. What have you to say?"

Sitting ever more stiffly in his seat, Michael was ramrod straight by the time he was done and flushed a dull red. "All true," he said, voice flat.

"Do I have your apology then?"

"Certainly not." The words came out as shot from a musket.

Daniel nodded, moving his last piece into place. "Very well, then, St. James. I demand satisfaction. Name your weapon."

Clearly, Michael thought Daniel had lost his mind. "You're challenging me to a duel. You, challenging me? Are you mad?"

"I suppose I must be. They do say unrequited passion will do that."

"Oh, don't be melodramatic."

"Surely I have as much right to it as you, my dear St. James." Daniel rose and made his way to the corner to avail himself of the chamber pot before washing his hands and face. Pulling on his clothes, he studied Michael out of the corner of his eye. He'd reduced the poor man to muttering to himself.

"Me! He challenges me when he knows I never miss a shot."

"Michael!"

"What!"

"Your weapon?"

"But we have no seconds. Nor do we have a doctor."

"I have no anticipation of requiring a sawbones. As for seconds, do you really wish to involve someone else?"

Shaking his head, Michael leaned back and looked at him, arms akimbo. "Very, well. Pistols. Closest shot wins. If I win, you let me go and do not follow."

How that stung. He would not show it, but hurt it did. "And if I win, you stay with me."

"Even if I do not wish to?"

"You do, Michael. You simply will not admit it. I assume you have your dueling pistols?"

"Yes."

Dawn saw them in a field outside of the town proper, both packed and ready to flee in case their activities drew the attention of the authorities, dueling being illegal, after all. They oiled and loaded the pistols, and were checking them a final time when Michael put a hand over his, stopping his methodical motions.

"Daniel, I... Why? You know it is by far better to let me go."

"You think it is because you are afraid. Just as I said before." Daniel leaned forward and kissed the corner of Michael's mouth. "I love you. I cannot let you leave me. Shall we pace it off?"

He waited, hoping against hope that Michael would declare all of the nonsense unnecessary, and Michael stared at him, long and hard. Then turned without a word and carefully counted out ten paces and waited for Daniel to do the same. It broke something in Daniel to see it, and he paced off his own distance with dull disinterest. He had pursued this course of action in hopes of provoking a reaction in Michael, hopes of forcing a declaration. Obviously he was foiled by Michael's stubborn nature.

Or perhaps he'd simply been wrong all along.

Michael took aim and was waited for him, hand rock steady, eye keenly sighted. Daniel almost fired his shot into the ground, a traditional surrender, but it was not in his nature to go quietly. So he lined up his shot and waited as well. And almost imperceptible nod from Michael, and they both pulled the trigger, and Daniel waited for the shot to hit, if not his body, than at least on the ground near him. More than a full minute passed before he realized that while his shot had been on the mark, digging a furrow into Michael's left coat sleeve, Michael's shot had been almost six feet wide. Deliberately.

He reached Michael's side just in time to catch him as he crumpled, taking them both to their knees on the wet ground. The wound was superficial, just as he'd supposed, Michael's collapse precipitated by strong emotion. Daniel lifted Michael's chin gently, looking into those well-loved eyes and seeing all of the things he had scarce hoped for.

"It seems you are right, Calhoun. I cannot leave you, no matter the cost."

"You let me win."

"I love you. Of course I did."

Elated, Daniel kissed him fiercely, pulling back only when Michael hissed in pain as Daniel's hand caught his injury. Running his fingers lightly over the scrape, Daniel smiled. "I've marked you as mine, now, St. James. There will be no going back. No running off. Not even if you think it best for me. Do you understand?"

"Yes. I think I do, finally."

"Good."

Michael could not fathom it. For all of Daniel's protests before he left, he really thought that when he did leave, the man would settle back into bucolic gentility and find some country lass and have babies, perhaps thinking of him fondly now and again. Oh, he'd known Daniel would look for him, but he had been careful to make it difficult and had assumed Daniel would give up long before now.

His arm throbbed in time with his heartbeat. Daniel had shot him. In order to keep him. Even more amazing, he had fired his own shot to miss. Deliberately.

Really, Michael could not believe it. 'Twas a duel that had ended the life he had known with his mother and father, forcing him to leave, forcing him to Virginia in the first place. Now, it seemed it was a duel that set him on yet another path, one where he would find a life with Daniel, one new to both of them, and adventure rather than an exile.

He looked to where Daniel stood in front of the basin, washing blood off his hands after bandaging Michael's wound. The innkeeper had seemed bemused to see them back so soon, but the room was still available, and had gladly rented it out to them again, deliberately not looking at Michael's dripping coat.

"You astound me, Daniel."

Daniel merely smiled benignly. "I know. I do not even need try too hard. Oh, by the by, I brought your pearls with me."

His mother's pearls. It had hurt him so to leave them behind. "They are yours now."

"Nonsense." Daniel came to sit beside him on the bed, irresistible with his bare, wet chest and low-slung trousers. "I intend to take the price out of your hide."

Delighted, Michael threw back his head and laughed. "Of course you do." He sobered, meeting Daniel's eyes with complete seriousness. "All that I am is yours."

Ever so gently, Daniel touched the score on his arm. "Mine indeed. Oh, you may wonder what Elias will do now."

Of course he wondered. He hoped… "Yes? Is

he well provided for?"

"He is the new overseer of my old estate. Jane assures me they will rub along well. He is a most capable sort."

"Excellent." Truly marvelous.

"Yes, and we must go and collect your horse. I bought him back on the road, and he is boarding until we can go and get him."

"Daniel." Michael turned blindly, his eyes filling as he reached for the man who had once been a mere distraction but had somehow become his world. "I do not deserve you."

The sound that came from Daniel's chest was part laugh, part sob, and those arms closed tight about him in return.

"No, St. James, you do not. But you will. I have every faith you will become the gentleman of substance you show the promise of being. Every faith indeed.

Epilogue

The day was warm, the late spring weather delightfully refreshing, the skies clear. Maryland had turned out to be a good compromise for him and Daniel, and the view grew upon him every day.

There could be no more perfect a day to take a long ride, and Michael had done just that. His stallion wanted to run, and he let him have his head, watching the countryside flash by, taking fences with reckless abandon. There were times when he mourned his old life, the things he went without to have a peaceful existence with Daniel, but at times like this he missed it not at all.

The fields and trees flashed by, and soon enough it was time to turn back to their little cottage, with its spring fed cold room and its big bed. Simple living. Who would have thought he could love it so?

By the time he got back to their small barn and walked his blowing mount out to cool him down, he was exhilarated, alive, and thrilled to be so. Even more thrilled when he saw Daniel Calhoun, stripped to the waist, wearing those bloody thin trousers he loved so, strong back sheened with sweat. The man was a god, truly, and he belonged to Michael. What a heady feeling.

He stabled Solomon and walked up behind Calhoun in time to see him stretch his whole torso, arms going over his head, muscles bunching and pulling. Michael's mouth went dry. Utterly lovely. He reached out to touch, only then realizing he still held his riding crop in his hand. Mischief bloomed in him, and he traced the line of Daniel's spine with the supple leather whip, stopping at the low waist of the trousers, lingering there.

Calhoun rumbled, looking back over his broad shoulder. "I do hope that is Michael St. James behind me, else I will be forced to hurt whomever it is."

"Why, yes, I believe I am he," Michael replied and stroked the tip of the whip back over the path it had traveled, up rather than down. Daniel shivered.

"Oh, well, that is all to the good then." Daniel turned to him, reaching, and Michael playfully batted at the man's hands with his crop.

"Yes. Very good indeed. You are a fine piece of flesh, you know. Enchanting." He watched, almost as from outside himself, as the crop slid along Daniel's jaw to his throat, then down over that wide chest to circle a tiny nipple. It hardened under the touch of the supple leather, and Michael smiled. So responsive, his Daniel, so perfectly beautiful.

Daniel actually blushed, and he grabbed the tip of the whip. "A fine piece, eh? Your smile tells me you have dishonorable intentions, St. James. Perhaps we should move indoors?"

"Whatever for?" Pulling the crop away, Michael resumed his exploration. "'Tis not as if we must concern ourselves with nosy neighbors or indiscreet servants. We have neither. At any rate, the setting suits you."

"Horse manure and rough wood stalls? How can I ever thank you for such a compliment?"

The crop smacked lightly against Daniel's belly. "No. The outdoors. The hard work, which produces a shine on your skin which I adore." As if his hand belonged to someone else, Michael watched it move, dragging the crop across the button placket of Daniel's breeches before sliding it between his legs, stroking the man's balls.

Those mossy green eyes fastened on his, wicked and daring. Those broad hands he so admired dropped to Daniel's breeches and started on the buttons. "Really? Then perhaps I will accommodate you and let you see all of me in my most natural setting."

Each piece of exposed skin felt the caress of Michael's crop, tickling and teasing as the trousers came down those muscled legs. When Daniel bent to pull off his boots, Michael moved, taking in the view from behind, flicking the crop between the man's beautifully rounded arse cheeks. "Oh, what a fine idea that is, Calhoun."

A strangled sound issued from Daniel's throat, the man teetering dangerously. A hand to his hip steadied him while the boots came off, and once Daniel stood naked before him, Michael took time to savor the feel of warm skin and firm muscle beneath his hand. The other hand maintained its hold on the whip, and he rubbed the shaft of it between Daniel's legs from the rear, pressing against sensitive spots unmercifully.

"St. James! That is...obscene."

"Delightfully so. You find it distasteful?"

"No." The strain in Daniel's voice was answered with a matching tension in his big body. "I simply fail to see why you...oh." The lush moan Daniel trailed off with made Michael's cock jump, as did the sight of the whip handle against the opening of Daniel's body.

"Fail to see what?" he paused.

"Nothing. Good Lord, St. James, do not stop now."

Michael smiled, snapping the whip in the air. "Go brace yourself on that stall door, Calhoun, while I find the oil. Spread yourself for me."

The muscles in Daniel's back jumped and twitched, but he did as he was bid, leaning his arms atop the stall door Michael indicated and spreading his legs, planting his feet wide apart. Verily, he was a man sculpted by a great master of Greek art, beautifully proportioned, utterly entrancing.

Collecting the oil from a shelf by the stable door, Michael opened it and spread a liberal portion over the handle of the crop. The sleek black leather gleamed, and the thought of it disappearing into Daniel's body excited him almost unbearably. He took the oil with him, tucking it in the hollow of his elbow so he could hold the whip in that hand and use the other to undo his breeches. They were far too tight.

When he touched the oiled crop against Daniel's lower back the man jumped, legs shifting, balls swaying. Mouth dry, heart pounding, Michael poured more oil, this time onto his fingers, and pressed them against Daniel's opening. He would simply ease the way a bit. Daniel took him easily, his fingers sliding into a hot, velvety vise.

"Oh, Daniel. So unbelievably good."

Daniel looked at him over one shoulder, dark green eyes glassy. "Only for you, St. James."

"Yes." Without further preparation, Michael pressed the stiff handle of the crop against the tight muscle guarding Daniel's body, pushing inside as smoothly as he could. A harsh sound escaped his throat at the sight, and Daniel arched his back, opening more fully to the invasion. Would that he never tired of this man. Of the things they might do together. He stroked Daniel's back, soothing both Calhoun and himself with the feel of that warm satin skin under his fingers. "I love you, Daniel."

Calhoun simply moaned once more, moving

his hips, taking more of the slick, black leather inside him, and Michael gave him what he needed, pushing it strongly into the man's body, using his other slick hand to stroke Daniel's shaft, pumping it roughly. Crying out, Daniel rocked between the two sensations, sweat beading between his shoulder blades, dripping down his back. Michael licked at it, tasting salt and desperation, purely sexual. The taste made his prick twitch, made him crowd closer, so that he might rub against Daniel's hip.

The sounds Daniel made were more addictive than opium. Michael forced the whip deeper while pulling at Daniel's foreskin, encouraging more of them. Daniel went up on his toes, low growls leaving his throat. Finally, head shaking side to side, Daniel began to beg.

"You, Michael. Should be you, there. Inside."

"Yes. Oh, yes, Calhoun." With one quick twist of his wrist Michael withdrew the whip, tossing it aside. The oil was still nearby, and he used it on his own aching cock, making ready with a few quick pumps. Daniel was ready for him, ripe for a good, hard ride. His back was wet with sweat, hair curling with it, arse red and open, legs shaking. Far too much for him to resist.

Michael pushed into Daniel's body with no more warning than a sharp grunt, and it jolted Daniel all the way through, so Michael felt the vibrations around his own flesh. They moved together in an agony of desperation, hot and needy. Daniel's cock throbbed in his hand, and the man's great form shook, and a hoarse cry escaped Daniel's throat, and it was rushing to a finish.

When hot fluid filled his hand, and tight muscles clamped about him, Michael all but screamed, plunging deep one last time to shudder and shake and give himself once more into Daniel's care. Where he knew he was always safe.

Leaning against Daniel's back, Michael permitted himself a rueful grin. Who was he to mourn his old life as he had earlier? Daniel Calhoun provided all of the excitement he could stand, and all of the moral fiber as well.

He was happy to be Daniel's rakehell. And to let Daniel be the gentleman of substance.

A Gentleman of Substance

Afterword

Hey, there! If you made it here, that means you finished Daniel and Michael's story, and I'm incredibly pleased you stuck around to the end! I wrote this book a long while back, and it's been a ball to revisit it and clean it up a bit. When I wrote Gentleman I was writing only erotic romance, where most of the action and characterization advanced through sexual situations.

Don't get me wrong, I still write a lot of sex and I still believe erotic romance is all about stripping people down to their most vulnerable and finding the humanity there inside the animal acts of sex. But I found as I went through Gentleman I was expanding scenes and adding in small scenes in between the existing ones so the focus expanded.

While ultimately I only added a couple thousand words to the story, and it's still very much an erotic romance, I think the book flows better, and I'm happier with the end result. Thank you so much for sharing Michael and Daniel with me, and I hope you loved them as much as I do.

XXOO
Julia Talbot
www.juliatalbot.com